STORIES IN TIME

AMERICA'S STORY

ACTIVITY BOOK

HARCOURT BRACE & COMPANY

Orlando Atlanta Austin Boston San Francisco Chicago Dallas

New York Toronto London

For permission to reprint copyrighted material, grateful acknowledgment is made to the following sources:

Chelsea House Publishers, a division of Main Line Book Co.: From "If You Miss Me from the Back of the Bus" in *Songs of Protest and Civil Rights*, compiled by Jerry Silverman. Lyrics copyright © 1992 by Chelsea House Publishers, a division of Main Line Book Co.

Dutton Children's Books, a division of Penguin Books USA Inc.: From *Immigrant Kids* by Russell Freedman. Text copyright © 1980 by Russell Freedman.

HarperCollins Publishers: From *Frontier Living* by Edwin Tunis. Text copyright © 1961 by Edwin Tunis.

McGraw-Hill, Inc.: From #60660 *The Log of Christopher Columbus* by Robert H. Fuson. Text copyright 1987 by Robert H. Fuson. Original English language edition published by International Marine Publishing Company, Camden, ME.

Printed in the United States of America

ISBN 0-15-303573-0

4 5 6 7 8 9 10 085 99 98 97

The activities in this book reinforce or extend social studies concepts and skills in **AMERICA'S STORY.** There is one activity for each lesson and skill. Reproductions of the activity pages appear with answers in the Teacher's Edition.

CONTENTS

UNIT 3

Chapter 5

Chapter 6

UNIT 4

Chapter 7

Chapter 8

UNIT 8

UNIT 9

A Native American Belief

Understand Oral History

DIRECTIONS: Read the following quotation. It describes what some Native Americans believe about their origins and their rights. Then answer the questions that follow.

"When we were created we were given our ground to live on and from this time these were our rights. This is all true. We were put here by the Creator—I was not brought from a foreign country and did not come here. I was put here by the Creator."

—*Chief Weninock, Yakima, 1915*

1. According to this quotation, where did the first Americans come from?

_____

2. Which sentence in the passage disagrees with the theory that the first Americans came across the Bering Strait? _____

_____

3. In the passage, what does "these were our rights" refer to? _____

_____

_____

4. What can you conclude about Native Americans' beliefs about land rights?

_____

_____

5. Why do you think Chief Weninock felt that he needed to state "This is all true"?

_____

_____

Harcourt Brace School Publishers

HOW TO USE A MAP to show movement

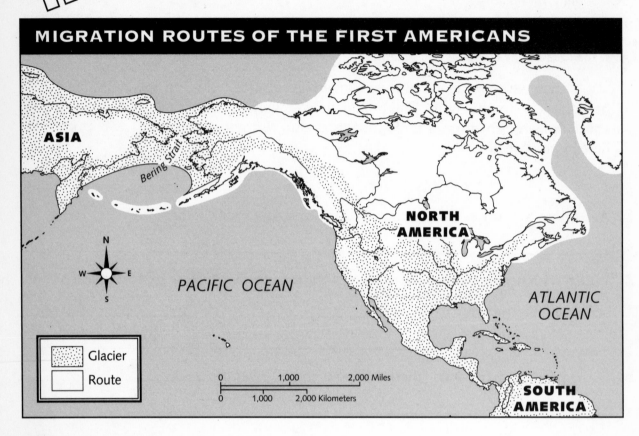

MIGRATION ROUTES OF THE FIRST AMERICANS

ASIA

Bering Strait

NORTH AMERICA

PACIFIC OCEAN

ATLANTIC OCEAN

SOUTH AMERICA

Glacier
Route

0   1,000   2,000 Miles
0   1,000   2,000 Kilometers

Apply Map Skills

DIRECTIONS: Use the map above and the map on page 38 in your textbook to complete these activities.

1. Scientists think the great migration lasted thousands of years. Use the compass rose to help draw the routes the first Americans used from Asia into and through the Americas. Use arrows to show direction. Use a colored pencil to fill in the key with the color and symbol you used for the routes.

2. In what direction did the first Americans who traveled toward South America move? In what direction did those who traveled toward Florida move?

_____

3. The first Americans hunted huge Ice Age animals for food and followed them over the glaciers. Color the glaciers in the Americas and Asia, and fill in the key for glacier with the same color. Then label the land bridge called Beringia.

Use after reading Chapter 1, Skill Lesson, pages 42–43.

Harcourt Brace School Publishers

THINK LIKE an Archaeologist

An archaeologist uses artifacts to learn about past cultures. Archaeologists are trained to find clues from artifacts in order to learn about a culture. They are also trained to know what clues artifacts do NOT give.

Club
Made from wood.
Used for hunting.

Bone Needle
Made from an animal bone splinter. Used to sew hides into clothing and tents.

Basket
Woven in different ways for different purposes. Used for gathering, preparing, and storing food.

Pottery
Handmade by coiling thin rolls of clay on top of one another. Used for storage and cooking.

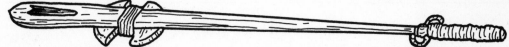

Atlatl
Spear-throwing weapon made of wood.

Learn from Visuals

DIRECTIONS: Write the name of the artifact or artifacts shown above that best answers the following questions.

1. Which artifact would have been the best to use to hunt the woolly mammoth?

_____

2. Which artifact shows that Native Americans made clothing? _____

3. Which two artifacts show that the Native Americans were food gatherers and farmers?

_____

4. Which three artifacts show that the Native Americans worked with crafts?

_____

5. Which two artifacts could have been used for cooking? _____

HOW TO RECOGNIZE Time Patterns on a Time Line

Apply Time Line Skills

DIRECTIONS: *Each of the six statements that follows tells how many years ago an event occurred. For each one, change the number of years shown to a calendar date using B.C. To change, or convert, from number of years ago to a B.C. date, subtract 2,000. Write these dates in the spaces provided. Then write the question number of each event above the correct date on the time line.*

1. The land bridge theory says the first people arrived in the Americas about

12,000 years ago. _____

2. Artifacts from about 13,000 years ago have been found in Monte Verde, Chile.

_____

3. Clovis points were first made about 11,600 years ago.

_____

4. Giant mammals became extinct in the Americas about 10,000 years ago.

_____

5. The last Ice Age ended about 10,000 years ago.

_____

6. Farming was practiced in central Mexico 7,000 years ago.

_____

| 11,000 B.C. | 10,000 B.C. | 9000 B.C. | 8000 B.C. | 7000 B.C. | 6000 B.C. | 5000 B.C. | 4000 B.C. |

Harcourt Brace School Publishers

Use after reading Chapter 1, Skill Lesson, page 51.

Preserving Native American Artifacts

Read Information in a Chart

**DIRECTIONS: The following chart lists some of the best-preserved
sites of early Native Americans in North America. Use the information
in the chart to answer the questions that follow.**

SITES OF NATIVE AMERICAN ARTIFACTS

NAME OF SITE	LOCATION	SIZE	FAST FACTS
Chaco Canyon National Historical Park	Bloomfield, New Mexico	33 sq miles (85 sq km)	Contains 18 major ruins dating from about A.D. 920 to A.D. 1130. Pueblo Bonito (meaning "beautiful town") was one of the largest Native American apartment-style houses. It was about 5 stories high, had 800 rooms and 32 circular kivas, and housed more than 1,200 people.
Effigy Mounds National Monument	Near Marquette, Iowa	2 sq miles (5 sq km)	Has burial mounds shaped like birds and animals. The Mound Builder people were active from about 1000 B.C. to about A.D. 1500.
Mesa Verde National Park	Southwestern Colorado	53,036 acres	Occupied from about A.D. 1 to about A.D. 1300. One pueblo, the Cliff Palace, held up to 1,000 people and had 200 rooms. Abandoned about two centuries before Europeans arrived in the Americas.
Petrified Forest National Park	Near Holbrook, Arizona	93,493 acres	Occupied A.D. 500 and remained occupied for 1,000 years. Preserves Native American petroglyphs (rock carvings) and prehistoric ruins.

1. At which site can you see burial mounds shaped like animals?

_____

2. At which site can you find one of the largest apartment-style houses?

_____

3. At which site can you see petroglyphs? _____

4. Which site is not located in the southwestern part of the United States?

_____

5. Which site is the oldest? _____

The First AMERICANS

Connect Main Ideas

DIRECTIONS: Use this organizer to show that you understand how the chapter's main ideas are connected. Complete the organizer by writing three details to support each main idea.

The First Americans

The environment affected the ways early peoples moved from place to place.

1. _____

2. _____

3. _____

The Environment

The ancient Indians coped with changes in their environment.

1. _____

_____

_____

2. _____

_____

_____

3. _____

_____

_____

Early peoples living in different parts of the Americas had different ways of life.

1. _____

_____

_____

2. _____

_____

_____

3. _____

_____

_____

Harcourt Brace School Publishers

Use after reading Chapter 1, pages 36–59.

NAME _____ DATE _____

TWO Northwest Coast Indian Canoes

The Northwest Coast Indians used dugout canoes with two different shapes. One type of canoe was built by the Haida. The other was built by the Nootka. Although the canoes were shaped differently, the methods and materials used to make them were the same. Both dugouts were made of white cedar. The largest canoes were more than 60 feet (18 m) long and as much as 8 feet (2 m) wide.

Compare Diagrams

DIRECTIONS: Compare the diagrams of the two types of canoes. Then answer the questions that follow.

HAIDA

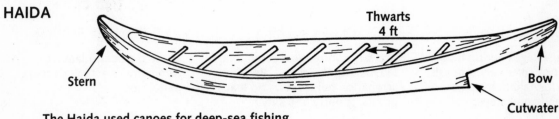

The Haida used canoes for deep-sea fishing.
All Haida canoes had high ends to make them more seaworthy.

NOOTKA

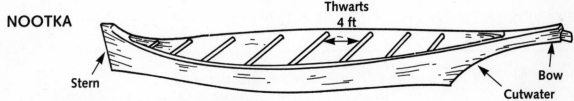

The Nootka used canoes for whaling.
All Nootka canoes had a flat strip on the bottom to keep them upright during whale hunts.

1. For what purpose was the Haida canoe used? _____

2. For what purpose was the Nootka canoe used? _____

3. Look at the bows, or the front ends, of the two canoes. How are they different?

_____

4. Now compare the sterns, or the back ends, of the two canoes. How are they different?

_____

5. The thwarts, or braces, that run across the canoes held the canoes' sides in place.

How far apart are the thwarts? _____

Learning About Kachinas

Interpret Visuals

DIRECTIONS: Study the drawings and descriptions of the three kachinas. Then answer the questions that follow.

Sun Kachina

Visits Hopi villages during the bean-planting ceremony. Appeals to the sun for health, happiness, long life, and good crops.

Clown Kachina

Appears during most ceremonies to entertain the crowd. Performs acrobatics, tells jokes, and leads games. Is noisy and silly.

Kachina Mother

Leads the bean-planting ceremony. Is actually a male performer.

1. Which kachina is a spirit of nature? _____

2. How can you tell one kind of kachina from another? _____

_____

3. Which part of the Sun Kachina's costume represents the sun?

_____

4. What makes the Clown Kachina's costume different from the other kachinas' costumes?

_____

_____

5. Which kachina do you think would play the most important role at the bean-planting

ceremony? Explain. _____

Harcourt Brace School Publishers

The Importance of the BUFFALO

The buffalo played an important part in the history of our country. As long as the buffalo roamed the Great Plains, the Plains Indians grew in number and strength. The people of the Plains hunted the buffalo for food and used other parts of the animal to make clothing, tools, weapons, and other products.

Read a Product Chart

DIRECTIONS: Study the chart below, which shows the most common buffalo products. Then answer the questions that follow.

BUFFALO PRODUCTS

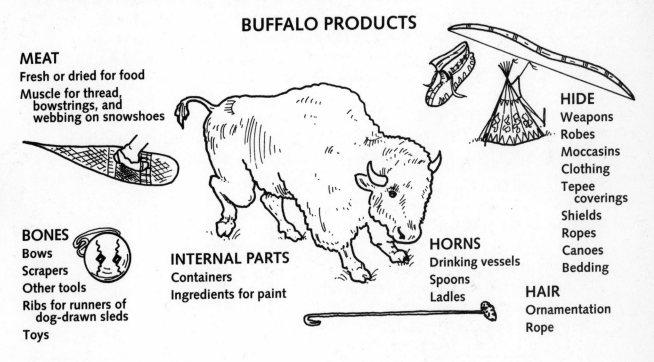

MEAT
Fresh or dried for food
Muscle for thread, bowstrings, and webbing on snowshoes

HIDE
Weapons
Robes
Moccasins
Clothing
Tepee coverings
Shields
Ropes
Canoes
Bedding

BONES
Bows
Scrapers
Other tools
Ribs for runners of dog-drawn sleds
Toys

INTERNAL PARTS
Containers
Ingredients for paint

HORNS
Drinking vessels
Spoons
Ladles

HAIR
Ornamentation
Rope

1. What did the Plains Indians make from the internal parts of the buffalo?

_____

2. Which three parts of the buffalo were used to make different kinds of weapons?

_____

3. Which part of the buffalo was used to make housing for the Plains Indians?

_____

4. Which part of the buffalo do you think made the most useful products?

_____

Harcourt Brace School Publishers

HIAWATHA & Longfellow Make History

Relate Literature to History

DIRECTIONS: Study the information about Hiawatha and the lines from Longfellow's poem. Then answer the questions.

Hiawatha, an Onondaga chief, worked hard for peace. In the late 1500s, he persuaded war-weary tribes of the Iroquois nation to stop fighting one another. They united in peace by forming what became known as the Iroquois League.

Hiawatha was believed to have been a shaman, or a religious leader and healer who calls upon the gods to grant the people special favors. He was said to have magical powers. Native American stories describe Hiawatha as a great teacher who taught valuable lessons about farming, hunting, canoeing, medicine, nature, and the arts.

Many years after Hiawatha's death, the stories about Hiawatha inspired Henry Wadsworth Longfellow to write the poem "The Song of Hiawatha." It took Longfellow from June 1854 to March 1855 to write it! You may recognize some verses from this lengthy poem. The lines that follow are from the section about Hiawatha's fasting, a time when he deliberately ate very little or nothing at all.

> "You shall hear how Hiawatha
> Prayed and fasted in the forest,
> Not for greater skill in hunting,
> Not for greater craft in fishing,
> Not for triumphs in the battle,
> And renown [fame] among the warriors,
> But for profit of the people,
> For advantage of the nations."

1. What was Hiawatha's major accomplishment? _____

_____

2. What is a shaman? _____

_____

3. Why do you think Longfellow was inspired to write a poem about Hiawatha?

_____

4. According to the poem, what was the purpose of Hiawatha's fasting?

_____

_____

Use after reading Chapter 2, Lesson 4, pages 75–78.

Harcourt Brace School Publishers

HOW TO IDENTIFY CAUSES and their EFFECTS

Most scientists believe the first Americans crossed over a land bridge from Asia to the Americas. This great migration lasted thousands of years. What was the cause of this great migration? What were the effects?

Apply Thinking Skills

DIRECTIONS: Use the information in Unit 1 about the great migration to complete the following flowchart. Use the flowchart on page 79 of your textbook as a guide.

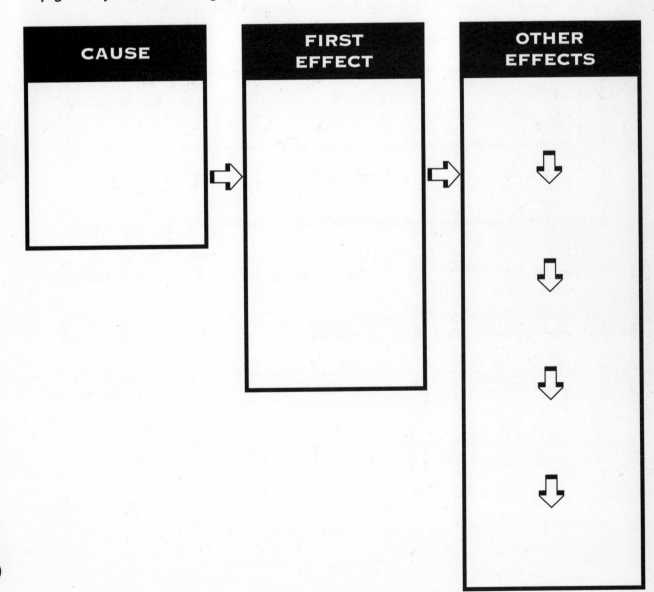

CAUSE

FIRST EFFECT

OTHER EFFECTS

Use after reading Chapter 2, Skill Lesson, page 79.

NAME _____ DATE _____

Unlocking the Mystery of
MAYAN NUMBERS

The Mayas built one of the most well-developed civilizations in the Americas. Their civilization was so developed that they had a system for writing and recording time. The Mayas' time system was based on their number system, which used three basic symbols. A shell stood for zero, a dot stood for one, and a bar stood for five.

Find Patterns

DIRECTIONS: Study the diagram that shows how the Mayas used three basic symbols in their number system. Then, using Arabic numerals, which is how we write our numbers, write the numeral that each Mayan symbol or group of symbols represents.

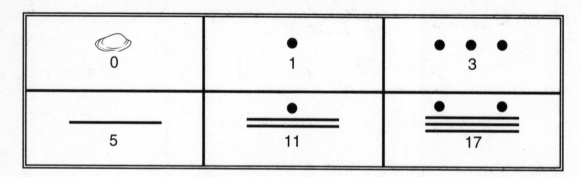

1. ___ ● ● ●

2. ___ ● ● ● ●

3. ___

4. ___

5. ___

6. ___

7. ___

8. ___

9. ___

10. Write your age using the Mayan number system. _____

Use after reading Chapter 2, Lesson 5, pages 80–85.

Harcourt Brace School Publishers

NAME _____ DATE _____

Indian Lifeways IN NORTH AMERICA

Connect Main Ideas

DIRECTIONS: Use this organizer to show that you understand how the chapter's main ideas are connected. Complete the organizer by writing three examples for each cultural region to show the diversity of Indian peoples.

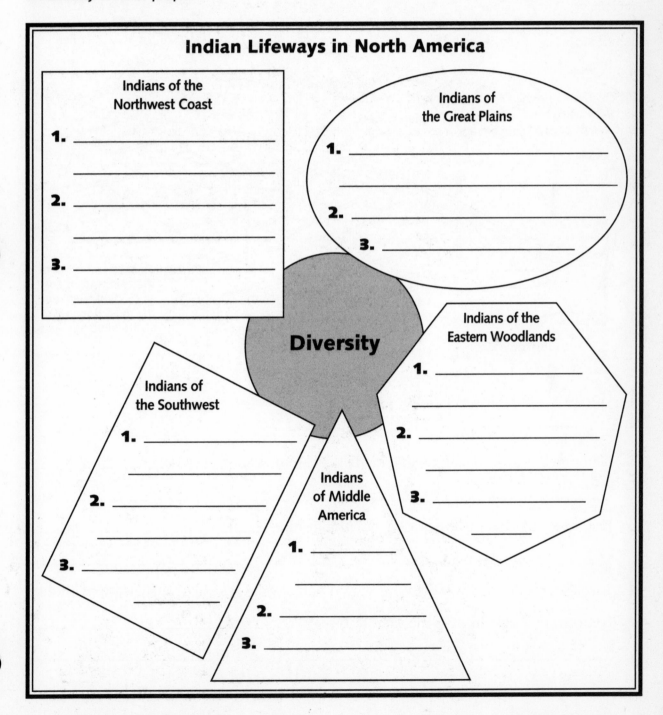

Indian Lifeways in North America

Indians of the Northwest Coast

1. _____
_____
2. _____
_____
3. _____
_____

Indians of the Great Plains

1. _____
_____
2. _____
3. _____

Diversity

Indians of the Eastern Woodlands

1. _____
_____
2. _____
3. _____
_____

Indians of the Southwest

1. _____
_____
2. _____
_____
3. _____
_____

Indians of Middle America

1. _____
_____
2. _____
3. _____

A $\mathcal{U}$ IKING $\mathcal{S}$ HIP

The Vikings were daring sailors. They set sail without compasses against strong winds and currents. They sailed in open ships such as the one shown below.

Learn Through Visuals

DIRECTIONS: Study the diagram below to answer the questions that follow.

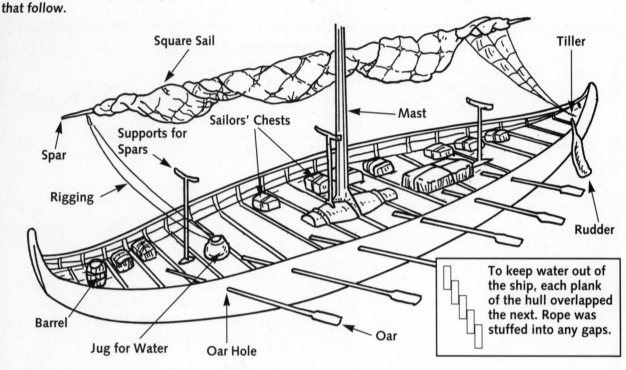

Square Sail · Mast · Tiller · Sailors' Chests · Spar · Supports for Spars · Rigging · Barrel · Jug for Water · Oar Hole · Oar · Rudder

To keep water out of the ship, each plank of the hull overlapped the next. Rope was stuffed into any gaps.

1. How was the Viking ship made watertight? _____

_____

2. Name two sources of energy that made the ship move. _____

_____

3. List three adjectives that describe the Viking ship. _____

_____

4. If you were a Viking, what reasons would you have to set sail in such a ship without a

compass or a map to cross the Atlantic Ocean? _____

_____

Use after reading Chapter 3, Lesson 1, pages 99–102.

Harcourt Brace School Publishers

MARCO POLO
and the Riches of Asia

Apply Thinking Skills

DIRECTIONS: Examine the goods that Marco Polo saw in Asia. Then complete the following activities.

Gunpowder

Used in war but also for fireworks

Number _____

Bookmaking Process

Stamping process used in China before it was developed in Europe

Number _____

Saffron

Used for color, to flavor food, and as a natural dye

Number _____

Silk

Silk threads produced by silk-worms and woven into fabrics

Number _____

"Black Stones"

(believed to be coal)
Used for fuel

Number _____

Jewels

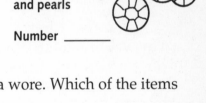

Diamonds, rubies, emeralds, and pearls

Number _____

1. Marco Polo was impressed with things the people in Asia wore. Which of the items above did Asians wear to show their great wealth? _____

2. In the spaces provided, label the goods from 1 to 6, with 1 being the item you think most encouraged Europeans to find new routes to Asia and 6 being the item you think least encouraged them.

3. If you had been a trader in the 1400s, which of the goods would have encouraged you to look for a route to Asia? Explain why you chose this item. _____

_____

Harcourt Brace School Publishers

Use after reading Chapter 3, Lesson 2, pages 103–107.

The Log of
CHRISTOPHER COLUMBUS

Columbus's log shows that he was aware of more than just the sea. His original log, which was given to the king and queen of Spain, was lost. But a copy, passed down from Columbus to his sons and grandson, is our link to Columbus's original log.

Interpret Primary Sources

DIRECTIONS: Read the following accounts from Columbus's log. Then answer the questions that follow.

Thursday, 20 September, 1492. Very early this morning three little birds flew over the ship, singing as they went, and flew away as the sun rose. This was a comforting thought, for unlike the large waterbirds, these little birds could not have come from far off.

Sunday, 23 September, 1492. I saw a dove, a tern, another small river bird and some white birds. . . . The crew is still grumbling about the wind. When I get a wind from the southwest or west it is inconstant, and that, along with a flat sea, has led the men to believe that we will never get home.

Monday, 24 September, 1492. I am having serious trouble with the crew. . . . They have said that it is insanity . . . on their part to risk their lives following the madness of a foreigner. . . . I am told by a few trusted men (and these are few in number!) that if I persist in going onward, the best course of action will be to throw me into the sea some night.

1. Why was Columbus comforted when he saw the little birds?

_____

2. Use context clues to find the definition of *inconstant*. In your own words, what does

inconstant mean? _____

_____

3. Why would an inconstant wind make the crew believe that they would not get home?

_____

4. Imagine being on board Columbus's ship. On a separate sheet of paper, rewrite the three entries from Columbus's log as though you were one of the crew.

Harcourt Brace School Publishers

HOW TO USE Latitude and Longitude

Columbus was an experienced sailor when he began his search for a new water route to Asia. His first voyage after settling in Portugal appears to have been in early 1477. The map shows some of his other early voyages.

Apply Map Skills

DIRECTIONS: On the map, study the voyages Columbus made before 1492. Then complete the activities.

1. Columbus set sail from Lisbon on each of his early voyages. Circle this city on the map.

2. What is Lisbon's location? Use longitude and latitude in your answer.

   _____

3. Put an **X** through Columbus's southernmost landing.

4. Draw a box around the landings that are located between 40°N and 60°N latitude.

5. Historians believe that Columbus landed in Iceland in 1477. At that time most people thought Iceland's northernmost point was at 63°N latitude. Columbus's landing proved otherwise. On the map locate Iceland's northernmost point and write the correct latitude in the space provided.

   _____

6. What name do we give this special

   parallel? _____

7. Between which two meridians were

   Columbus's landings? _____

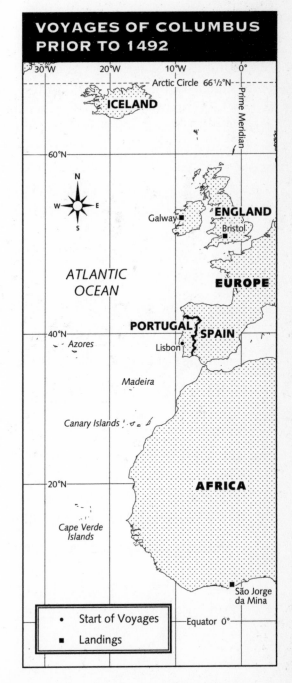

VOYAGES OF COLUMBUS PRIOR TO 1492

- Start of Voyages
- Landings

Harcourt Brace School Publishers

The Costs of EXPLORATION

Compare Costs

DIRECTIONS: *Read the information below and study the comparison table. Then complete the activities that follow.*

How can we understand the costs of Columbus's voyage when prices and values have changed over the centuries? One way is to compare costs by using the value of gold. The maravedi was a copper coin used in Spain in the 1400s. Each maravedi would have about a value of just over 13 cents. The table at the right shows the costs of the first voyage in maravedis and United States dollars.

COSTS OF COLUMBUS'S VOYAGE OF DISCOVERY

	MARAVEDIS	U.S. DOLLARS*
Salaries of all officers	268,000	34,840
Wages of all sailors	252,000	32,760
Maintenance	319,680	41,558
Rental cost, *Santa Maria*	172,800	22,464
Furnishings, arms, trading supplies	155,062	20,158
Total Expenses	**1,167,542**	**151,780**

*maravedis × $0.13 = U.S. dollars

1. Put a dollar sign ($) next to the most expensive part of the voyage. Then put an **X** next to the least expensive part of the voyage.

2. Compare the salaries of the officers and the wages of the sailors. Did it cost more to pay the officers or the sailors? Circle the one that cost more.

3. Columbus offered a reward of 10,000 maravedis to the first person to sight land. What

   is this amount in U.S. dollars? _____

   _____

4. The average yearly wage of a sailor on Columbus's voyage was 3,000 maravedis, or $390. Columbus's yearly salary was 50,000 maravedis, or $6,500. If you were a sailor on Columbus's voyage, considering your average yearly wages, would the 10,000 maravedi reward make you want to continue to look for land? (Columbus

   eventually claimed the reward for himself.) Explain. _____

   _____

   _____

Harcourt Brace School Publishers

Use after reading Chapter 3, Lesson 4, pages 114–118.

NAME _____ DATE _____

HOW TO FORM A Logical Conclusion

Columbus died believing that he had reached Asia. Other explorers, however, proved him wrong. Among those explorers were Vespucci, Balboa, and Magellan. These explorers found new facts to prove that Columbus had landed on a different continent.

Apply Thinking Skills

DIRECTIONS: *Decide which explorer could have made each statement below. In the space provided, write a V for Vespucci, a B for Balboa, or an M for Magellan. Then draw an X through any statement that does not support the conclusion that these explorers had landed on a different continent.*

1. _____ I found a new way of measuring east and west distances on a map.

2. _____ I was Portuguese, sailing under the Spanish flag.

3. _____ I was killed in a fight on the Philippine Islands.

4. _____ I learned that I had sailed more than three times as far as Columbus thought he had sailed.

5. _____ Many of my crew died of scurvy and hunger.

6. _____ I found a huge ocean on the western side of what Columbus had thought was Asia.

7. _____ I climbed a mountain peak on the Isthmus of Panama.

8. _____ I studied Ptolemy's work and found that if Asia were as far east as Columbus had thought, it would cover half the Earth.

9. _____ In the areas I explored, I saw no evidence of what Marco Polo had seen in Asia.

10. _____ I found that you could reach Asia by sailing west around the world.

11. _____ I supported Vespucci's findings by crossing the Isthmus of Panama.

12. _____ My ships sailed for more than three months across the Pacific.

13. _____ My exploring party included Spanish and African soldiers.

14. _____ I set sail in September 1519.

Harcourt Brace School Publishers

The Age of
Exploration

Connect Main Ideas

DIRECTIONS: Use this organizer to show that you understand how the chapter's main ideas are connected. Complete the organizer by writing three examples to support each main idea.

The Age of Exploration

Europeans learned information about the outside world.

1. _____
2. _____
   _____
3. _____

New Information

Changing conditions led Europeans to explore unknown lands in the 1400s.

1. _____
2. _____
3. _____

New Information

Columbus landed in what he thought was Asia.

1. _____
2. _____
3. _____

New Information

The facts gathered by later explorers changed how people thought about the voyages of Columbus.

1. _____
2. _____
3. _____
   _____

Use after reading Chapter 3, pages 98–121.

Harcourt Brace School Publishers

A Day in TENOCHTITLÁN

What was it like to live in the Aztec capital of Tenochtitlán before it was conquered by Cortés? Here is an account of what a typical day for a male citizen in that city might have been like.

Understand Other Cultures

DIRECTIONS: Read the story about daily life in Tenochtitlán. Complete the table that follows to compare your daily life with that of an Aztec living in Tenochtitlán.

The merchant's guild has accepted me as a member. I am now ready to travel with a caravan of my own. How my life will change!

The temple trumpets guide the daily routine in Tenochtitlán. My stucco house has one bedroom for the whole family, one other small room, a bathroom, and no furniture except mats. At sunrise the sound of the temple trumpets wakes me and I bathe, put on my loin cloth, pick up food to eat later, and go to work. Before long I hear the trumpets again. Then I take the day's first meal and return to work. At about the time the sun is directly overhead, the trumpets signal me to return home to eat and to take a brief nap. After my nap, I go back to work until nightfall, when the trumpets sound the end of the workday.

At the end of the workday, I go home and spend time with my family until the trumpets blow again. Then I know it is time to go to sleep.

	YOU	AZTEC
Wake-Up Time		
Housing		
Meals		
Work		

Harcourt Brace School Publishers

Use after reading Chapter 4, Lesson 1, pages 123–126.

Estéban in Time and Place

Sequence Events

DIRECTIONS: Read the following quotations about Estéban. Place the events discussed in the proper sequence by numbering the passages from 1 to 5, with 1 being the first event and 5 the last. Then use the information to answer the questions that follow.

_____ "In 1538 Governor Mendoza organized an expedition to discover this land of great wealth and picked Father Marcos de Niza, a Franciscan friar, to lead it. Estéban was his advance scout and advisor." *William Loren Katz*

_____ "Estéban traveled ahead of the main group, taking only a few Indians with him. The Indians could not speak Spanish, so Estéban agreed to send Friar Marcos a cross made of twigs or tree branches to report his findings. A small cross would mean he had found nothing out of the ordinary. But if he found great cities he would send back a large cross." *Sibyl Hancock*

_____ "Some historians, unfriendly toward the African, . . . [believe] he was murdered. One scholar believes Estéban died for claiming to represent a powerful white country to Indians. Some historians have wondered if the young slave saw an opportunity for freedom and took it." *William Loren Katz*

_____ "Not too much is known of his [Estéban's] early life. Born in Azamore, Morocco, around 1500, he was probably made captive as a teenager when Portugal's King Manoel seized the city in 1513." *William Loren Katz*

_____ "Estéban . . . proceeded into the interior and sent back wooden crosses to indicate his progress. When his crosses increased in size until they were as tall as a man, the Spaniards realized that the [African] explorer had experienced great success. Indians brought news of Little Stephen's [Estéban's] approach to the fabulous seven cities about which so much had been heard." *John Hope Franklin*

1. In what country was Estéban born? _____

2. Who was chosen to lead the expedition? _____

3. List all of Estéban's jobs. _____

4. Reread Katz's different descriptions of Estéban's death. On a separate sheet of paper, write your own ending to the story of Estéban's search for the Seven Cities of Gold.

Do You Speak *Spanish?*

Understand Word Origins

DIRECTIONS: Study the information in the box below. Use your textbook to help you fill in the blanks in the dictionary box. Then answer the questions that follow.

alligator   came to English through Spanish. The Spanish word for "alligator" is *lagarto*. The Spanish word for "the" is *el*. When English speakers heard *el lagarto*, it sounded to them like "alligator."

armadillo   is a Spanish word meaning "armed man," or "little armored one." This word describes an animal whose body is almost entirely protected by an armorlike covering.

_____ comes from the Spanish word meaning one who takes control by physical, mental, or moral force.

The name for the state of

_____ comes from the Spanish word meaning "filled with flowers."

mosquito   is a Spanish and Portuguese word that simply means "little fly."

parakeet   comes from the Spanish *periquito* and the Old French *paroquet*, "parrot."

1. What part of speech are all of these words? _____

2. Which word came to English through a misunderstanding? _____

3. Which words came to English from two different languages? _____

4. Which Spanish word is the name of a state? _____

5. On a separate sheet of paper, make a list of all the words you know that come from Spanish.

6. On the same sheet of paper, make a table with the following headings: ANIMALS, PEOPLE, PLACES. Write the words from the dictionary box and the words from the list you made for question 5 under the proper headings. Circle the category heading under which you have the most words.

Harcourt Brace School Publishers

Preparing **Furs** for **Trade**

The French bartered with the American Indians, exchanging European goods for beaver furs. At first the French did not hunt the beaver. American Indians trapped the beavers and prepared the beaver skins, or pelts, for trade.

Read a Flowchart

DIRECTIONS: Study the flowchart that shows the steps American Indians followed to tan and cure beaver skins. Then answer the questions that follow.

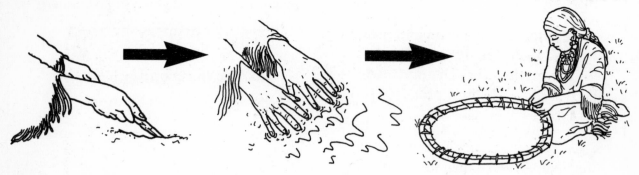

Step 1
Scraping: Scraping the pelt with a stick to clean it

Step 2
Tanning: Rubbing the pelt with marrow (sticky center of bone)

Step 3
Curing: Drying the scraped and marrow-rubbed pelt on a stretching frame

1. What was the first step in preparing the beaver skins for trade?

_____

2. Describe the tanning process. _____

_____

3. What was the final step in preparing the hide for trade? _____

_____

_____

4. Rewrite these steps in the correct order: tanning, scraping, curing.

_____

Use after reading Chapter 4, Lesson 4, pages 135–138.

Harcourt Brace School Publishers

HARVEST FESTIVALS

Was the Pilgrims' Thanksgiving the first Thanksgiving? You already know that there are many ideas about the first Thanksgiving in the Americas. What about the rest of the world? People around the world have held harvest festivals since they first harvested crops.

Compare Holiday Celebrations

DIRECTIONS: Study the chart below to learn about harvest festivals around the world. Next, complete the chart by filling in the information for the United States. Then use the chart to complete the activities that follow.

HARVEST FESTIVALS

PLACE	NAME OF FESTIVAL	WHEN HELD	FESTIVITIES
India	In honor of Gauri, goddess of the harvest and women	September	Offerings of milk and sweets to Gauri; feasting
Israel	Sukkot (also called the Feast of Tabernacles)	Autumn	Special shelters called succahs or tabernacles are built
Ancient China	Hhung-Ch'iu (the birthday of the moon)	Fifteenth day of the eighth month	Round moon cakes and round fruits on altars
England	Harvest Home	Harvest time; autumn	Feasting on roast beef, pudding; songs
Inca Empire	The Song of the Harvest	May (autumn in Southern Hemisphere)	Offering of first corn to their gods
United States			

1. During which season of the year are most harvest festivals held?

_____

2. Why do you think the Incas celebrated their harvest festival in May?

_____

_____

3. On a separate sheet of paper, describe what you think would be the perfect Thanksgiving Day celebration, from the beginning of the day to the end.

Harcourt Brace School Publishers

Use after reading Chapter 4, Lesson 5, pages 139–144.

HOW TO READ a Vertical Time Line

Apply Time Line Skills

DIRECTIONS: The time line on the next page lists events that happened in many different places. Study the time line and then complete the activities below.

1. In which year was the lead pencil first manufactured? _____

2. In which country were checks, or "cash letters," first used? _____

3. Which event occurred first—Diego Velázquez's completion of the painting *The Water Carrier of Seville*, or Leonardo da Vinci's death? _____

4. How many years passed between the death of the last Viking in Greenland and the birth of the first English child in North America? _____

5. Label the events on the left side of this time line, "Events Happening in North America," and those on the right, "Events Happening in Other Places."

6. Four events are incorrectly listed on the "Events Happening in Other Places" side of the time line. Circle these events and draw arrows from the circles to the correct spot on the other side of the time line.

7. Use your textbook to fill in the blank spaces on the "Events Happening in North America" side of the time line.

8. What was happening in North America in the same year that Diego Velázquez completed his famous painting? _____

Harcourt Brace School Publishers

(Continued)

Use after reading Chapter 4, Skill Lesson, page 145.

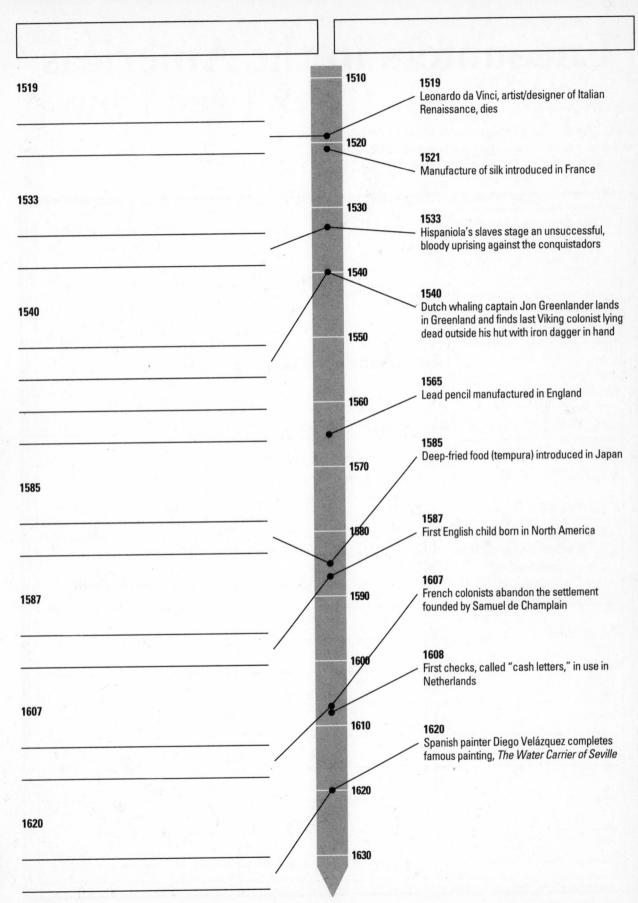

1519

_____

_____

1533

_____

_____

1540

_____

_____

_____

1585

_____

_____

1587

_____

_____

1607

_____

_____

1620

_____

_____

1510

1519
Leonardo da Vinci, artist/designer of Italian Renaissance, dies

1520

1521
Manufacture of silk introduced in France

1530

1533
Hispaniola's slaves stage an unsuccessful, bloody uprising against the conquistadors

1540

1540
Dutch whaling captain Jon Greenlander lands in Greenland and finds last Viking colonist lying dead outside his hut with iron dagger in hand

1550

1565
Lead pencil manufactured in England

1560

1585
Deep-fried food (tempura) introduced in Japan

1570

1587
First English child born in North America

1580

1590

1607
French colonists abandon the settlement founded by Samuel de Champlain

1600

1608
First checks, called "cash letters," in use in Netherlands

1610

1620
Spanish painter Diego Velázquez completes famous painting, *The Water Carrier of Seville*

1620

1630

Use after reading Chapter 4, Skill Lesson, page 145.

Encounters in the Americas

Connect Main Ideas

DIRECTIONS: Use this organizer to show that you understand how the chapter's main ideas are connected. Complete the organizer by writing the main idea of each lesson.

The Conquest of the Aztecs and Incas

_____
_____
_____
_____
_____
_____
_____
_____

Indians

Europeans

Africans

Encounters in the Americas

The English in the Americas

_____
_____
_____
_____
_____
_____
_____
_____

The Search for Gold and Riches

_____
_____
_____
_____
_____
_____
_____

Settlers and Slaves

_____
_____
_____
_____
_____
_____
_____

Encounters with the French and Dutch

_____
_____
_____
_____
_____
_____
_____

Harcourt Brace School Publishers

Use after reading Chapter 4, pages 122–147.

Comparing Spanish Missions

The mission of San Antonio de Valero was built by the Catholic church in what is now Texas. This mission was later given a new name—Pueblo del Alamo, later known as the Alamo.

Understand Diagrams

DIRECTIONS: Compare the diagram below with the diagram of a California mission shown on page 161 in your textbook. Write a **C** next to each statement that describes a California mission. Write an **A** next to each statement that describes the Alamo. Write **CA** next to each statement that describes both missions.

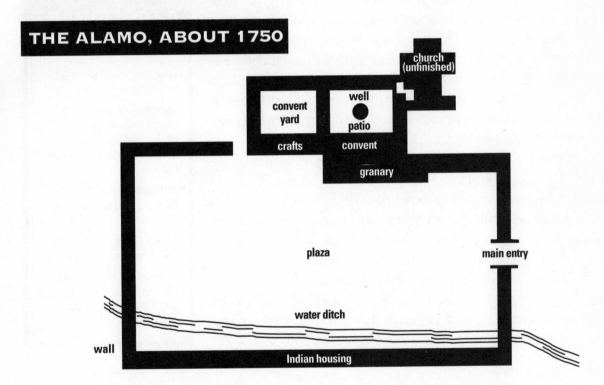

THE ALAMO, ABOUT 1750

_____ water source outside mission

_____ all crafts contained within mission walls

_____ large, open area in center of mission

_____ mission includes a church

_____ missionaries housed inside mission

_____ ranch workers housed outside mission

_____ walls surround entire mission

_____ patio within mission walls

Use after reading Chapter 5, Lesson 1, pages 159–163.

a taste of
LOUISIANA

Apply Language Arts Skills

DIRECTIONS: Study the list of words in the box and read the
passage about Louisiana below. Then write the correct word for
each numbered blank on the lines following the passage.

Welcome to Louisiana, a spicy, southern state
splashed by the waters of the Gulf of Mexico. Water
dominates Louisiana. Slow-moving streams known as **1**
are common sights. The Mississippi River carries millions
of tons of sediment, or sand and soil, into the Gulf of
Mexico and deposits it at the mouth of the river, forming a
delta. The Mississippi Delta covers about one-fourth of the
state. The average Louisiana resident lives on land that is
five feet below sea level. Wetlands throughout Louisiana
are home to many kinds of wildlife. Herons, bald eagles,
and brown pelicans thrive there. Millions of ducks, geese,
and other birds winter in Louisiana. But the state is more
than colorful geographic features and birds. A multicultur-
al spirit flavors Louisiana! Treat yourself to the flavorful
local foods by eating a hot bowl of **2** or a spicy rice dish of
3. As you eat, listen for the street-side musicians playing
toe-tapping **4**. Visit New Orleans, where jazz was born,
and join in one of the many music festivals.

In New Orleans, excitement is in the air. People in the
street chat about the upcoming **5**, a fun-filled celebration
of music, costumes, and parades. Louisiana natives come
from all over the state to join in this celebration.

A DICTIONARY OF LOUISIANA

bayous slow-moving
streams

gumbo a spicy soup
made with a mixture
of vegetables, meat,
seafood, and sassafras
leaves

jambalaya spicy rice
cooked with seafood
or meat

Mardi Gras a day of
merrymaking and carnival

zydeco a type of music
that combines rock and roll
with Cajun and African
American sounds

1. _____

2. _____

3. _____

4. _____

5. _____

Use after reading Chapter 5, Lesson 2, pages 164–168.

Who AM I?

Identify Diverse Groups

DIRECTIONS: Read the following statements that might have been made by people living in the British colonies. Decide whether each statement best identifies a colonist from the southern, middle, or New England colonies. In the blank next to each statement, write S for southern colonist, M for middle colonist, or NE for New England colonist.

_____ **1.** I work for the Virginia Company and sell tobacco from the colonies to buyers all over Europe.

_____ **2.** I live in Plymouth. I came to North America because I wanted my religion to be more "pure."

_____ **3.** I live in a colony that originally had no plantations. This colony has good land, but its original charter outlawed bringing enslaved Africans to the colony.

_____ **4.** I settled in a colony that was founded as a refuge for Catholics.

_____ **5.** I started the settlement of Providence because I was driven out of Massachusetts.

_____ **6.** I am learning a lot from my Irish Catholic, German Lutheran, and Jewish neighbors.

_____ **7.** I run a trading post in New Sweden.

_____ **8.** I was in prison in England because I had huge debts. I came to this colony to work off my debt.

_____ **9.** I live in the "breadbasket" colonies.

_____**10.** I settled in this part of the colonies with a large number of other Huguenots.

_____**11.** I am the Reverend Thomas Hooker. I founded my own colony because I did not like the way the Puritan leaders controlled the Massachusetts colony.

_____**12.** I am a Quaker. I live in the colony founded by William Penn.

_____**13.** I hope my indigo plants will help my colony prosper.

_____**14.** I love living in Philadelphia. It has streets that form squares. This busy place is a main port for shipping and trading and for immigrants coming to settle in the colony.

Use after reading Chapter 5, Lesson 3, pages 169–176.

HOW TO USE a Table to Classify INFORMATION

Although the colonists lived in the Americas, they still thought of themselves as Spanish, Dutch, French, English, or African, depending on where they came from. These colonists brought with them the languages and customs of their homelands, and these languages and customs became part of our history. Their influences can still be seen throughout the United States today.

Apply Thinking Skills

DIRECTIONS: Examine the terms shown. Then decide whether the term was originally used by or identified with Spanish, French or English colonists. Write the term under the name of the appropriate category.

Juan Ponce de León	Des Moines	San Antonio	Puritans
Sir Francis Drake	El Camino Real	Code Noir	Quakers
King George II	Florida	hacienda	mission
La Salle	Jamestown	Huguenots	The Virginia
King Louis XIV	Louisiana	indigo	Company
St. Augustine	New Orleans	portage	Fundamental
Pedro Menéndez de Avilés	Quebec	presidio	Orders

SPANISH	FRENCH	ENGLISH

Harcourt Brace School Publishers

Use after reading Chapter 5, Skill Lesson, page 177.

Europeans Settle Throughout
NORTH AMERICA

Connect Main Ideas

DIRECTIONS: Use this organizer to show that you understand how the chapter's main ideas are connected. Complete the organizer by writing details about each main idea.

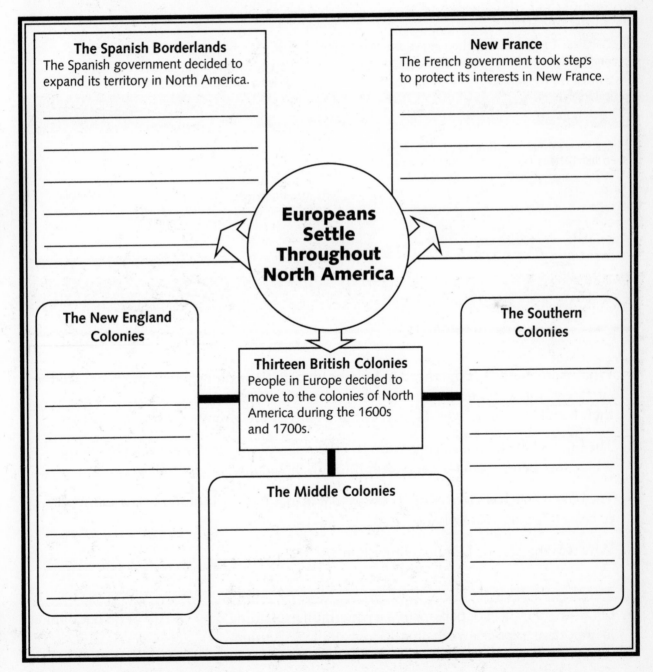

The Spanish Borderlands
The Spanish government decided to expand its territory in North America.

_____
_____
_____
_____
_____

New France
The French government took steps to protect its interests in New France.

_____
_____
_____

Europeans Settle Throughout North America

The New England Colonies

_____
_____
_____
_____
_____
_____
_____

Thirteen British Colonies
People in Europe decided to move to the colonies of North America during the 1600s and 1700s.

The Southern Colonies

_____
_____
_____
_____
_____
_____

The Middle Colonies

_____
_____
_____

Use after reading Chapter 5, pages 158–179.

Having a **WHALE** of a Time

New London, Connecticut; New Bedford, Massachusetts; and Sag Harbor, New York, were once important whaling centers. By the 1970s whalers had killed so many whales that many species were near extinction. In 1972 the United States Marine Mammal Protection Act stopped the widespread slaughter of whales by United States citizens. Many other countries have passed similar laws.

Link History to Science

DIRECTIONS: Use the information above and the diagram below to complete the activities following the diagram.

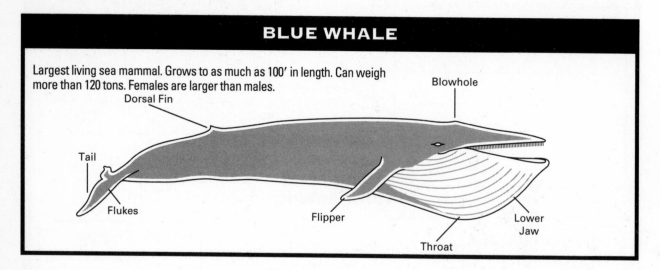

BLUE WHALE

Largest living sea mammal. Grows to as much as 100′ in length. Can weigh more than 120 tons. Females are larger than males.

Dorsal Fin · Blowhole · Tail · Flukes · Flipper · Throat · Lower Jaw

1. Whales are mammals that need to breathe air into their lungs. They must come to the surface of the water every few minutes to breathe. Whales' nostrils are in the top of their heads. Put an **X** over the part of the whale where you would find its nostrils.

2. The blue whale travels at speeds up to 15½ miles per hour. Circle each part of the whale that helps it balance and steer through the water.

3. The blue whale has grooves on its throat that help it trap mouthfuls of "sea soup." Shade or color this part of the whale.

4. Why was the Marine Mammal Protection Act passed? _____

_____

5. On a separate sheet of paper, write a paragraph explaining why you do or do not think it is important to pass laws that protect whales from hunters.

Use after reading Chapter 6, Lesson 1, pages 181–184.

NAME _____ DATE _____

HOW TO READ a Circle Graph

Apply Graph Skills

DIRECTIONS: Use the information in the chart and graph below to answer the questions that follow.

	UNITED STATES POPULATION IN 2050		
Key	**Nationality**	**%**	**Total Population**
|||||	Anglo American	52	202,000,000
	Hispanic American	21	81,000,000
	African American	16	62,000,000
	Asian American	10	41,000,000
	Native American	1	5,000,000

UNITED STATES POPULATION IN 2050

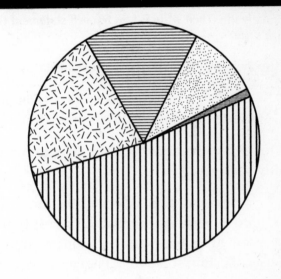

1. Which nationality will make up the largest percentage of the United States population in 2050? _____

2. Which nationality will make up the second-largest percentage of the population?

_____

3. Which group will make up the smallest percentage of the population?

_____

4. Compare this circle graph with the one on page 185 of your textbook, showing the population of colonial America. Use the circle graphs to make at least one generalization about changes in the population from colonial days to the year 2050.

_____

_____

Looking at Life in the Southern Colonies

Do you think you would be ready at age 17 to take over the business of three plantations? Eliza Lucas did just that. She did not have a choice. The Lucas family moved from the West Indies to South Carolina when Eliza was 16 years old. Soon after her father went off to fight a war, her mother fell seriously ill and Eliza was left in charge.

Describe Life on a Plantation

DIRECTIONS: *Study Eliza Lucas's own words. Try to understand her daily life. Then write E next to each statement that describes Eliza's life.*

After being left in charge of the plantations, Eliza wrote the following to a friend in England:

> "I have the business of three plantations to transact . . . [which] requires much writing and more business and fatigue of other sorts than you can imagine. "

After experiencing what it was like to run the three plantations, Eliza wrote of her daily routine:

> "I rise at five o'clock in the morning, read till seven, then take a walk in the garden or fields, see that the servants are at their respective business. . . . The first hour after breakfast is spent at music, the next is constantly employed in recollecting something I have learned, such as French or shorthand."

_____ **1.** I am tired from all the writing and business that is part of managing three plantations.

_____ **2.** I have basically the same daily routine as other teenagers.

_____ **3.** I spend much of the early morning reading.

_____ **4.** It is important to remember what you read and learn.

_____ **5.** No teenager is able to take charge of a business.

_____ **6.** I spend my whole day working and have no time for fun.

_____ **7.** It is important to be up before sunrise.

_____ **8.** Taking a walk in the garden or fields is a waste of time.

DIRECTIONS: *On a separate sheet of paper, write a brief description of your daily routine. How does your daily routine compare to Eliza Lucas's? Do you see life the same way?*

Use after reading Chapter 6, Lesson 2, pages 186–190.

TOOLING Around the Frontier

Sequence with Visuals

DIRECTIONS: The diagram below shows how the broadax was used to make lumber to build cabins. Study the diagram. Then place the steps on the right in the proper sequence by numbering them from 1 through 10.

USING THE BROADAX TO MAKE LUMBER

Step 1 Making chalk line on bark-stripped log. Four chalk lines are made by "twanging" a chalked cord onto log to square off log.

Chalk Line

_____ Strip bark.

_____ Snap chalk lines.

_____ Hew log to chalk lines.

_____ Stand on log and hold felling ax.

_____ Fell, or cut down, tree.

Step 2 Scoring to chalk line. Stand on log and hold long-handled felling ax. Use felling ax to make deep vertical cuts up to chalk line. This is known as "scoring."

Dog

Felling Ax

_____ Stand next to log and hold broadax.

_____ Place "dog" to hold log.

_____ Make vertical cuts in log.

_____ Place chalk lines on log.

Step 3 Hewing to chalk line. Stand alongside log. Hold broadax with two hands. Place one knee next to log. Use broadax to hew, or split off, the vertical cuts made in Step 2.

Broadax

_____ Notch ends of log to use to build cabin.

Use after reading Chapter 6, Lesson 3, pages 191–193.

HOW TO USE a Product Map to Make Generalizations

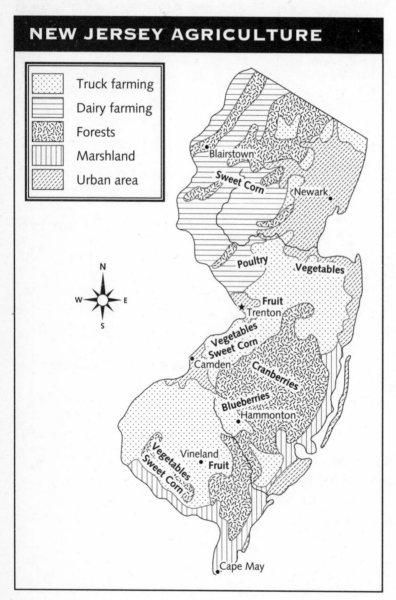

Apply Map Skills

DIRECTIONS: Use the map below to complete the following activities.

NEW JERSEY AGRICULTURE

Legend:
- Truck farming
- Dairy farming
- Forests
- Marshland
- Urban area

Blairstown
Sweet Corn
Newark
Poultry
Vegetables
Fruit
Trenton
Vegetables
Sweet Corn
Camden
Cranberries
Blueberries
Hammonton
Vegetables
Sweet Corn
Vineland
Fruit
Cape May

1. Draw a line from Newark to Cape May. Identify the different areas you would pass through if you traveled from north to south along this line.

_____

_____

2. What city in New Jersey is located in the area where cranberries and blueberries are grown?

_____

3. What is the main use of land around Vineland?

_____

4. What crop grows in most parts of New Jersey?

_____

5. Would you be more likely to be a farmer if you lived in Vineland, Cape May, or Newark?

_____

Use after reading Chapter 6, Skill Lesson, pages 194–195.

NAME _____ DATE _____

THE PEOPLE OF THE
BRITISH COLONIES

Connect Main Ideas

DIRECTIONS: Use this organizer to show that you understand how the chapter's main ideas are connected. Complete the organizer by writing details about each main idea.

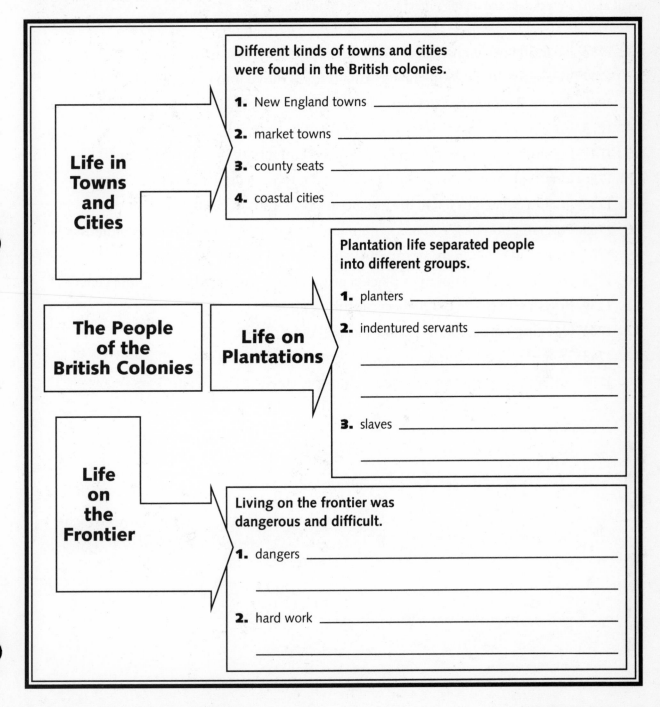

Life in Towns and Cities

Different kinds of towns and cities were found in the British colonies.

1. New England towns _____

2. market towns _____

3. county seats _____

4. coastal cities _____

The People of the British Colonies

Life on Plantations

Plantation life separated people into different groups.

1. planters _____

2. indentured servants _____

_____

_____

3. slaves _____

_____

Life on the Frontier

Living on the frontier was dangerous and difficult.

1. dangers _____

_____

2. hard work _____

_____

HISTORICAL EVENTS
OF THE 1700s

Sequence Dates on a Time Line

DIRECTIONS: Write the number of each event in the correct place on the time line. Make sure to place the number of the event at the correct date and on the correct side of the time line.

1. **1755** Earthquake shocks Lisbon, Portugal, killing at least 10,000 people

2. **1747** Virginia settlers and Pennsylvania traders move into Ohio Territory

3. **1760** Daniel Boone hired to scout the frontier in present-day eastern Tennessee

4. **1755** British drive French settlers out of Acadia

5. **1749** Philadelphia founds what becomes the University of Pennsylvania

6. **1726** Jonathan Swift's novel, *Gulliver's Travels,* is an instant success in Europe

7. **1750** Johann Sebastian Bach, the great composer, dies in Germany

8. **1763** Proclamation of 1763 bans settlement west of the Appalachian Mountains

9. **1753** French in Canada move into British lands in Ohio River valley

10. **1716** Dreaded pirate known as Blackbeard killed in sea battle off Virginia coast

11. **1759** British win Battle of Quebec, capturing city

12. **1754** Opening battle of French and Indian War

13. **1763** Treaty of Paris signed, ending the French and Indian War

14. **1756** British declare war on French in Europe, starting the Seven Years' War

NORTH AMERICA

| 1710 | 1720 | 1730 | 1740 | 1750 | 1760 | 1770 | 1780 |

OTHER PLACES

Use after reading Chapter 7, Lesson 1, pages 209–212.

HOW TO USE A Historical Map

Apply Map Skills

DIRECTIONS:
The map on this page shows where some large immigrant groups were concentrated during the colonial period. Study the map. Then answer the questions that follow.

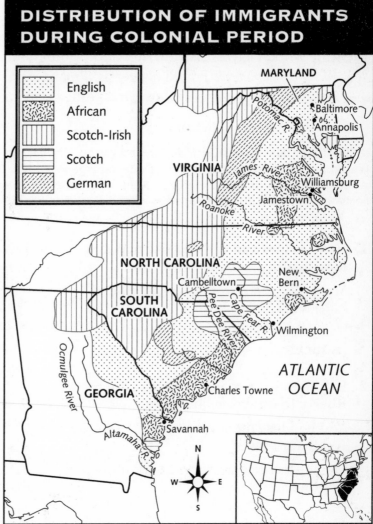

DISTRIBUTION OF IMMIGRANTS DURING COLONIAL PERIOD

English
African
Scotch-Irish
Scotch
German

MARYLAND
Baltimore
Annapolis
Potomac R.
VIRGINIA
James River
Williamsburg
Jamestown
Roanoke River
NORTH CAROLINA
Cambelltown
New Bern
Pee Dee River
Cape Fear R.
SOUTH CAROLINA
Wilmington
Ocmulgee River
ATLANTIC OCEAN
GEORGIA
Charles Towne
Altamaha R.
Savannah

1. Which immigrant group settled farthest west? _____

2. Which immigrant group settled farthest south? _____

3. Where did most of the Africans settle? _____

_____

4. Which immigrant groups settled in all of the southern colonies?

_____

UNDERSTANDING PROVERBS IN
Poor Richard's Almanack

Benjamin Franklin, a respected colonist, was and still is known for his political and scientific work. He was also a writer and printer who published a yearly almanac called *Poor Richard's Almanack*. Franklin's yearly almanacs were popular with the colonists because they contained a variety of features, including calendars, weather predictions, and recipes.

Analyze the Meaning of Proverbs

DIRECTIONS: Franklin also included proverbs in his almanac. A proverb is a short, commonly used saying that expresses a general truth. Below are some proverbs from Poor Richard's Almanack. Circle the statement below each proverb that best describes what the proverb means.

1. **Early to bed and early to rise makes a man healthy, wealthy, and wise.**

   You will benefit from good habits and hard work.

   You will be rich if you stick to your bedtime.

2. **Sell not virtue to purchase wealth, nor liberty to purchase power.**

   You will lose money if you try to buy wealth or power.

   Do not sacrifice your values for money or power.

3. **Don't throw stones at your neighbors, if your own windows are glass.**

   Do not criticize others, because you have faults, too.

   You can do what you want to others if you protect yourself first.

4. **Make haste slowly.**

   Consider your actions carefully.

   If you hurry, you can get more done.

5. **Tart words make no friends: a spoonful of honey will catch more flies than a gallon of vinegar.**

   Speak kindly to others and you will have many friends.

   You will make many friends if you feed them honey.

6. **Blessed is he that expects nothing, for he shall never be disappointed.**

   It's easy to achieve low goals.

   Set your goals high so you will not be disappointed.

7. **No gains without pains.**

   Life is hard.

   To get better at something, you must work hard at it.

8. **Being ignorant is not so much a shame as being unwilling to learn.**

   It is a waste not to be eager for an education.

   People who are not smart are sad.

Use after reading Chapter 7, Lesson 2, pages 216–221.

Harcourt Brace School Publishers

Events Leading to Revolution

Colonial printers turned out news sheets that often were hung in public places. These sheets told of events happening in the colonies.

Write Historical News Stories

DIRECTIONS: Imagine you are writing a news sheet in the colonies. For each date below, write a headline for and a description of an important historical event.

December 1773

_____
_____
_____
_____
_____
_____

April 18, 1775

_____
_____
_____
_____
_____
_____

September 1774

_____
_____
_____
_____
_____
_____

April 19, 1775

_____
_____
_____
_____
_____
_____

HOW TO MAKE Economic Choices

Apply Thinking Skills

DIRECTIONS: Imagine you have $20 to spend. Then complete the graphic organizer that follows to help you make an economic choice.

CHOICES
List three $20 items you would like to buy.

OPPORTUNITY COSTS
List the value each item has to you.

ECONOMIC CHOICE
Compare the value of what you will be giving up, or the opportunity costs, for each choice. What are you willing to give up, or trade off? Make an economic choice based on which item will best meet your needs with the $20 you have to spend. List that item below. Your other choices become your trade-offs.

Use after reading Chapter 7, Skill Lesson, page 227.

DIFFERENCES DIVIDE
Britain and Its Colonies

Connect Main Ideas

DIRECTIONS: Use this organizer to show that you understand how the chapter's main ideas are connected. Complete the organizer by writing three details to support each main idea.

Britain Rules the Colonies → **Differences Divide Britain and Its Colonies** → **Britain and the Colonies Go to War**

Government in the Colonies
The British colonists became unhappy with British rule.

1. _____
_____
2. _____
_____
3. _____
_____

Quarrels over Taxes and Government
Individuals and groups in the British colonies worked to make changes in their government.

1. _____
_____
2. _____
_____
3. _____
_____

The Colonists Unite
The colonists came together as they protested British rule.

1. _____
_____
_____
2. _____
_____
3. _____
_____

The Redcoats
ARE COMING!

Compare Visuals

DIRECTIONS: Compare the drawings of the British soldier's uniform and the Continental soldier's uniform. Then write C next to each statement below that describes a Continental uniform. Write B next to each statement that describes a British uniform. Write CB next to each statement that describes both uniforms.

Continental Uniform

Cheap, easy to sew

Small pack for supplies

Homemade hunting shirt

Gray-brown trousers

Boots with no left or right foot

British Uniform (Redcoat)

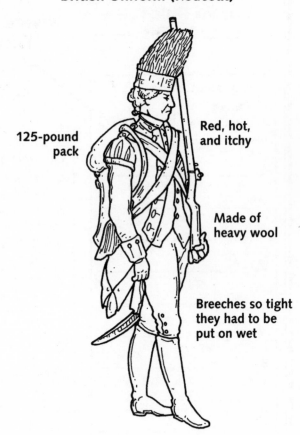

125-pound pack

Red, hot, and itchy

Made of heavy wool

Breeches so tight they had to be put on wet

_____ hard to tell if soldier bleeding

_____ most visible in woods

_____ included a musket

_____ included a pack

_____ most practical

_____ included a canteen

_____ knee-length boots

_____ fringed shirt

_____ three-cornered hat

_____ included an ax

HOW TO READ a Political Cartoon

Apply Visual Thinking Skills

DIRECTIONS: Examine the political cartoon below. Then answer the questions that follow.

NOVEMBER 1780
French General, Count De Rochambeau, Reviewing the French Troops in America

1. When was this political cartoon drawn? _____

2. The cartoon caption points out that the general was reviewing French troops in America. Why were there French troops in America? _____

_____

3. What conclusions can you draw about the cartoonist's opinion of the French soldiers?

_____

4. What specific items in the cartoon led you to your conclusion?

_____

_____

Men Wrote It,
But a Woman Printed It

Only men drafted and signed the Declaration of Independence. But a woman printed it! Why would a woman be chosen to print the official copy of the Declaration? Read the passage below to find out.

Read Line by Line for Comprehension

DIRECTIONS: Use the line numbers in the passage to help you answer the questions that follow.

1   The Declaration of Independence was signed on July 4, 1776. By January 1777, it had
2 been printed seven times! There was, however, no official copy of the Declaration.
3 So, on January 18, 1777, Congress decided to print official copies for each state in
4 the new union.
5   The members of Congress wanted to find a local printer. This meant that they would
6 look in Baltimore, because that was where they were meeting. (By then, the British had
7 taken Philadelphia.) The logical choice was Mary Katharine Goddard.
8   Goddard was well known and experienced. She had a reputation for being a high-
9 quality printer. Goddard had learned the printing trade from her brother. She printed
10 her own newspaper, the *Maryland Journal,* and had even been the head of the post office of
11 Baltimore since 1775!
12   How can you tell the difference between the Declaration that Goddard printed and the other
13 copies? The one Goddard printed lists the delegates' names in neat columns next to the
14 states they represented. On the very bottom of the document, you will find "Baltimore,
15 In Maryland: Printed by Mary Katharine Goddard."

1. Which line tells you the number of times the Declaration had been printed by

January 1777? _____

2. Which lines tell why Congress wanted to print official copies? _____

3. Lines 5–7 tell why the members of Congress wanted to find a printer in Baltimore.

What was their reason? _____

4. Reread lines 8–11. List the reasons Congress chose Goddard as the printer.

_____

5. List the line numbers of the paragraph that explains how to tell the difference between the

Declaration that Goddard printed and the other copies. _____

Harcourt Brace School Publishers

AMERICANS TAKE SIDES

Not all of the people living in the British colonies supported the fight for independence from Britain. About one third sided with the Loyalists, another third sided with the Patriots, and another third remained neutral.

Categorize Information

DIRECTIONS: Write the following names or groups of people in the appropriate category in the chart below. You may wish to reread pages 240–243 in your textbook.

Abigail Adams   Peter Salem
John Adams   Mary Slocumb
General Thomas Gage   Ethiopian Regiment
Patrick Henry   most Native Americans
Richard Henry Lee   many northern Anglicans
Peter Muhlenberg   many southern Presbyterians
John Murray   Quakers
Thomas Paine   Unmarried Ladies of America

LOYALIST	PATRIOT	NEUTRAL

Characterize Patriots

Map Characters in a Story

DIRECTIONS: Use the characters in Samuel's Choice to complete the organizer below. Describe each character's role by filling in the appropriate box.

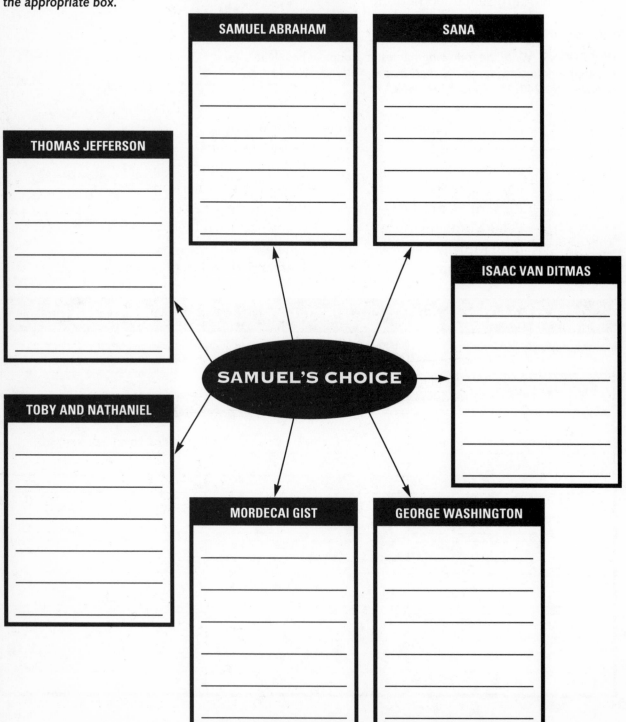

Use after reading Chapter 8, Lesson 4, pages 244–247.

Harcourt Brace School Publishers

Which Event Happened First?

Sequence Events

DIRECTIONS: In each pair of events of the American Revolution, circle the event that happened first.

1.	Committees of Correspondence formed	Second Continental Congress formed
2.	Second Continental Congress formed	Battle of Lexington and Concord
3.	Second Continental Congress formed	Olive Branch Petition sent to King George III
4.	Winter at Valley Forge	Battle of Bunker Hill
5.	Richard Henry Lee gives speech to Second Continental Congress declaring free and independent states	Thomas Paine's *Common Sense* published
6.	Jefferson plans the Declaration	Second Continental Congress formed
7.	George Washington's troops almost wiped out after winter at Valley Forge	Declaration of Independence signed
8.	Colonists' victory at Saratoga	French join Revolution on colonists' side
9.	Treaty of Paris signed in 1783	Battle of Yorktown
10.	Treaty of Paris signed in 1783	Benedict Arnold becomes a traitor

Use after reading Chapter 8, Lesson 5, pages 248–253.

The War for Independence

Connect Main Ideas

DIRECTIONS: Use this organizer to show that you understand how the chapter's main ideas are connected. Complete the organizer by writing the main idea of each lesson.

The War for Independence

At War with the Homeland →

_____
_____
_____
_____

The Decision for Independence →

_____
_____
_____
_____

Americans Take Sides →

_____
_____
_____
_____

The Push for Victory and Independence →

_____
_____
_____
_____

Use after reading Chapter 8, pages 230–255.

Articles of Confederation

The Articles of Confederation united 13 independent states. The Articles gave the national government certain powers, but because Americans wanted to guard their newly won freedom, the national government they formed was weak.

Identify Reasons

DIRECTIONS: Study the table below. It lists weaknesses of the Articles of Confederation. Complete the table by filling in a reason for each weakness.

WEAKNESS	REASON
There was no strong national government.	
At least 9 of the 13 states had to agree on any law or decision.	
No single leader controlled the government.	
Congress could not raise a national army without the permission of the states.	
Congress could not collect taxes.	
Congress could not make laws about trade.	

Use after reading Chapter 9, Lesson 1, pages 267–271.

Who Was There?

Identify Historical Figures

DIRECTIONS: From the list at the right, choose the person who might be describing his part in the Constitutional Convention. Write the letter identifying his name in the correct blank below.

A. John Adams
B. Patrick Henry
C. John Hancock
D. Thomas Jefferson
E. Daniel Shays
F. Benjamin Franklin
G. James Madison
H. Gouverneur Morris
I. George Washington
J. Samuel Adams

_____ **1.** In 1779 I was elected to represent Virginia as a member of Congress under the Articles of Confederation.

_____ **2.** I was elected president of the Constitutional Convention.

_____ **3.** I was sick, so I could not attend the Constitutional Convention.

_____ **4.** I refused to take part in the Constitutional Convention because I did not believe that a stronger national government was a good idea.

_____ **5.** I said of the Constitutional Convention, "It really is an assembly of demigods."

_____ **6.** I was Congress's youngest member at 29 years of age.

_____ **7.** I was carried to the Constitutional Convention in a Chinese sedan chair.

_____ **8.** I could not attend the Constitutional Convention because I was in Paris as the U.S. ambassador to France.

_____ **9.** I changed the opening words in the Preamble to the Constitution to read: *We the people of the United States. . . .*

_____ **10.** I could not attend the Constitutional Convention because I was in London as the U.S. ambassador to England.

_____ **11.** I was too busy as governor of Massachusetts to attend the Convention.

_____ **12.** As a frontier farmer, I was not invited to the Convention.

_____ **13.** I was given the job of writing down all the ideas that were approved during the Convention.

_____ **14.** I was the most honored hero of the American Revolution.

Use after reading Chapter 9, Lesson 2, pages 272–275.

NAME _____ DATE _____

HOW TO FIGURE
TRAVEL TIME AND DISTANCE

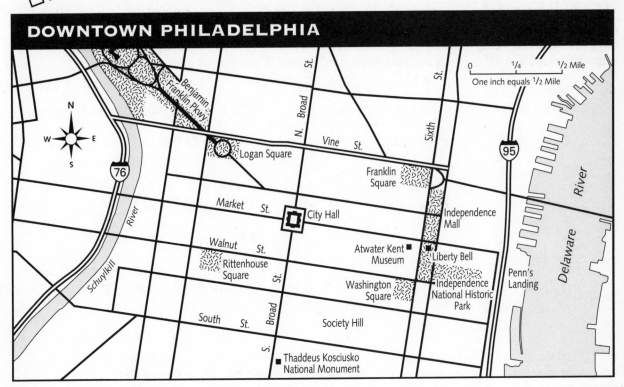

DOWNTOWN PHILADELPHIA

 Apply Map Skills

DIRECTIONS: Study the map above to complete the following activities.

1. Draw the following route on the map: You are at the Liberty Bell. Go west on Market Street to City Hall. Head south on S. Broad Street to Thaddeus Kosciusko National Monument.

2. On this map, 1 inch stands for ¹/₂ mile. Use a ruler to measure the number of inches

covered by the route you drew. Write your answer here. _____

3. Multiply the total number of inches traveled by ¹/₂ (the number of miles equal to 1 inch). This will tell you the total number of miles that would be traveled if you walked

this route in Philadelphia. _____

4. To find out how long it would take to travel this route at different speeds, divide the total number of miles by the rate of travel shown below.

Walking (3 mph): _____

Jogging (6 mph): _____

Use after reading Chapter 9, Skill Lesson, pages 276–277.

Who Has the Power?

Compare Government Systems

DIRECTIONS: Use the diagram on page 279 of your textbook and the information from Unit 5 to complete the following activities. Put an N next to powers that belong to the national government, an S next to powers that belong to state governments, and a B next to powers that are shared by both.

_____ **1.** Raise money by taxing citizens

_____ **2.** Set up public schools

_____ **3.** Set rules for state and local elections

_____ **4.** Print and coin money

_____ **5.** Raise an army and a navy

_____ **6.** Make treaties with other countries

_____ **7.** Control trade among states

_____ **8.** Control trade within states

_____ **9.** Set up courts

_____ **10.** Declare war

_____ **11.** Admit new states

_____ **12.** Make laws for marriage and divorce

DIRECTIONS: Compare the powers granted to the national government by the Constitution with those granted to it by the Articles of Confederation by completing the activities that follow. You may need to review Lesson 1 on the Articles of Confederation.

1. Put a check mark next to those powers of the national government that are the same under the Constitution as they were under the Articles of Confederation.

2. Circle the powers of the national government that are new under the Constitution.

3. Think about what your life might be like if the Articles of Confederation still governed the United States. Then use information summarized in the activities on this page to write a paragraph that explains why the Constitution made the United States a stronger country.

_____

_____

_____

_____

_____

Harcourt Brace School Publishers

Use after reading Chapter 9, Lesson 3, pages 278–282.

HOW TO COMPROMISE TO RESOLVE CONFLICTS

Apply Thinking Skills

DIRECTIONS: Complete the graphic organizer that follows. For each step, write in the arguments, decisions, or both made at the Constitutional Convention that led to the Great Compromise.

BOTH SIDES CLEARLY STATE WANTS AND NEEDS

BOTH SIDES UNDERSTAND WHAT IS TO BE GIVEN UP

BOTH SIDES DECIDE WHAT IS MOST IMPORTANT

BOTH SIDES DISCUSS POSSIBLE COMPROMISES

BOTH SIDES VOTE ON COMPROMISES

Harcourt Brace School Publishers

Use after reading Chapter 9, Skill Lesson, page 283.

Who Does What in
THE GOVERNMENT?

Diagram the U.S. Government

DIRECTIONS: Study the diagram on page 285 of your textbook that shows how a bill becomes a law. Then order the steps of the process below from 1 to 6.

_____ The bill becomes a law or is sent back to Congress for another vote.

_____ A member of the House or the Senate introduces a bill.

_____ The President reviews the bill.

_____ Congressional committees review the bill.

_____ The President either vetoes the bill or signs it into law.

_____ Both houses of Congress vote to approve the bill.

DIRECTIONS: Study the diagram on page 287 of your textbook that shows how checks and balances work. Then complete the chart below by writing in the branch that holds each particular power and the branch being checked. The first one has been completed for you.

BRANCH HOLDING AUTHORITY	CHECK/BALANCE	BRANCH BEING CHECKED
Legislative	Override the President's veto	Executive
	Appoint Supreme Court justices	
	Rule President's actions unconstitutional	
	Veto a bill	
	Approve treaties	
	Approve appointments of Supreme Court justices	

Harcourt Brace School Publishers

Use after reading Chapter 9, Lesson 4, pages 284–287.

Constitutional Footnotes

Understand a Primary Source

DIRECTIONS: Read the Preamble to the U.S. Constitution below. Then figure out what the footnoted, or numbered, words and phrases mean. Write the number of the footnote next to the best explanation.

We the people of the United States,
  in order to form a more perfect union,[1]
  establish justice,[2]
  insure domestic tranquility,[3]
  provide for the common defense,[4]
  promote the general welfare,[5] and
  secure the blessings of liberty[6]
  to ourselves[7]
  and our posterity,[8]
  do ordain,[9]
  and establish[10]
  this Constitution for the United States of America.

_____ **a.** set up a fair system

_____ **b.** set up

_____ **c.** make sure there is peace at home

_____ **d.** make a better government

_____ **e.** make official

_____ **f.** supply protection for all

_____ **g.** encourage health, happiness, and comfort

_____ **h.** gain and keep the gifts of freedom

_____ **i.** everyone who later becomes part of this country

_____ **j.** everyone belonging to this country

Use after reading Chapter 9, Lesson 5, pages 288–293.

NAME _____ DATE _____

The Constitution

Connect Main Ideas

DIRECTIONS: Use this organizer to show that you understand how the chapter's main ideas are connected. Complete the organizer by writing the main idea of each lesson and by describing the three branches of government.

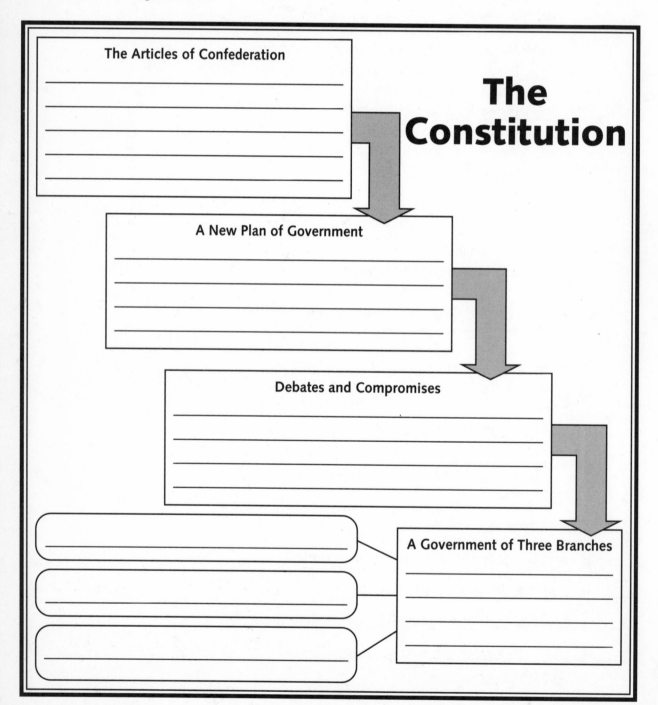

The Articles of Confederation

_____
_____
_____
_____

The Constitution

A New Plan of Government

_____
_____
_____
_____

Debates and Compromises

_____
_____
_____
_____

_____

_____

_____

A Government of Three Branches

_____
_____
_____

Use after reading Chapter 9, pages 266–295.

the MAZE of RATIFICATION

Sequence States

DIRECTIONS: Use the map and the table on page 299 of your textbook to get through the maze of ratification. Draw a line from Start to the first state to ratify the Constitution. Then continue through the maze to connect the remaining states in the order of their ratification.

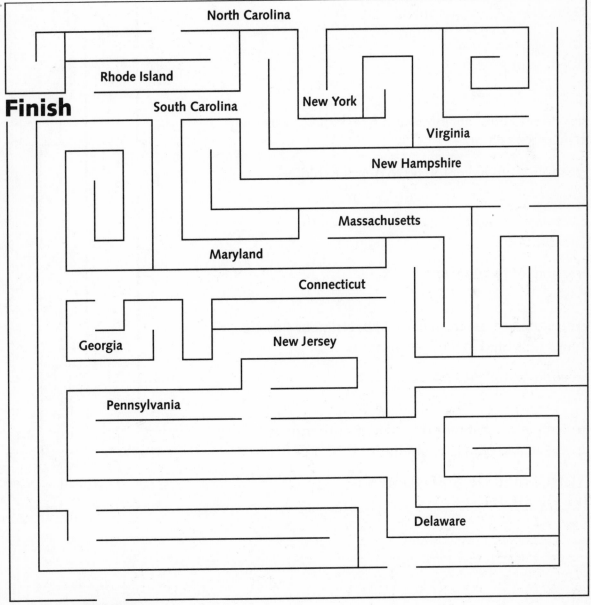

North Carolina

Rhode Island

Finish

South Carolina

New York

Virginia

New Hampshire

Massachusetts

Maryland

Connecticut

Georgia

New Jersey

Pennsylvania

Delaware

Start

Counting the Amendments

Number the Bill of Rights

DIRECTIONS: Read the list of freedoms below, and decide which amendment protects each one. Write the amendment's number in the box opposite each freedom. If all your answers are correct, you can add the numbers in each of the three columns and one of your totals will equal the number of amendments in the Bill of Rights. Circle the correct total.

1. Right to "keep and bear arms"

2. Right to a speedy and public trial

3. Freedom of speech

4. Freedom to hold meetings and to ask the government to hear complaints

5. Freedom from being forced to quarter soldiers

6. Protection of rights that are not listed in the Constitution

7. Freedom of religion

8. Protection against the national government's doing things not listed in the Constitution

9. Freedom of the press

10. Protection against the government's ordering an unreasonable search of a home

TOTAL NUMBER OF AMENDMENTS IN BILL OF RIGHTS

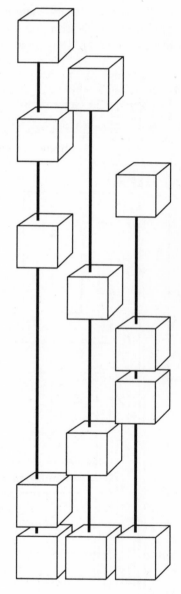

Harcourt Brace School Publishers

Use after reading Chapter 10, Lesson 2, pages 304–306.

NAME ______________________ DATE ____________

Who's in Office?

Organize Information

DIRECTIONS: Complete the following graphic organizer about the first U.S. government under the Constitution. Use the information in your textbook as a guide.

THE FIRST U.S. GOVERNMENT

EXECUTIVE BRANCH

President

____

Vice President

____

CABINET

Secretary of ______________ was ______________

Secretary of ______________ was ______________

Secretary of ______________ was ______________

Attorney ______________ was ______________

LEGISLATIVE BRANCH

The two houses

____

____

JUDICIAL BRANCH

Chief Justice

____

Use after reading Chapter 10, Lesson 3, pages 307–312.

HOW TO LEARN FROM A DOCUMENT

This résumé, or summary of experience, lists information Benjamin Banneker might have written about himself. The cover of Banneker's almanac lists information about his publication.

Résumé
BENJAMIN BANNEKER

- Born in Baltimore, Maryland, 1731

- Son of free Africans

- Learned to read from grandmother

- Self-taught in calculus and spherical trigonometry

- Aptitude for mechanical sciences

- Made first wooden clock in America

- First important African scientist in the United States

- Served for two years on the commission to survey and plan the city of Washington, D.C.

- Wrote and published annual almanac with at least 29 editions

Apply Thinking Skills

DIRECTIONS: Study the two documents above. Then complete the activities that follow.

1. Underline the title of Banneker's publication.

2. Circle the year in which Banneker's work was published.

3. Put a star next to the city in which Banneker's work was printed.

4. What do you think is Banneker's most interesting accomplishment? Explain why.

_____

_____

A New Government *Begins*

Connect Main Ideas

DIRECTIONS: Use this organizer to show that you understand how the chapter's main ideas are connected. Complete the organizer by writing the main idea of each lesson.

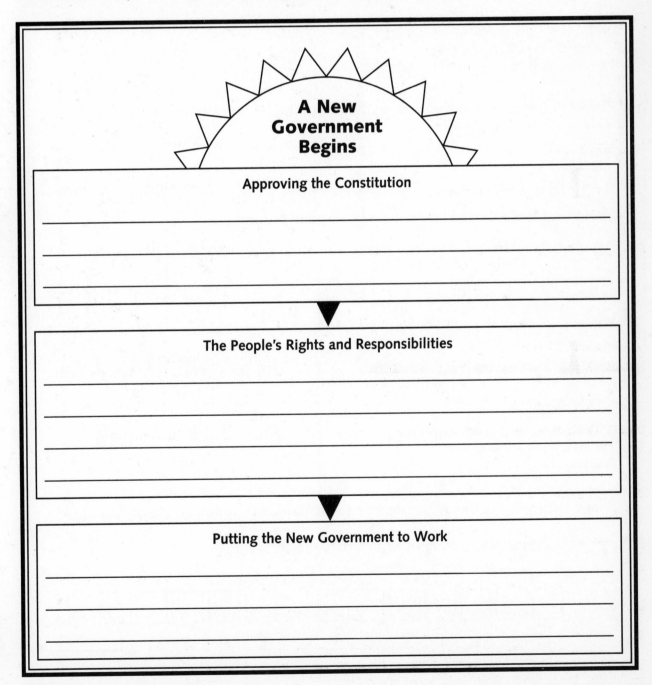

A New Government Begins

Approving the Constitution

_____

_____

_____

_____

▼

The People's Rights and Responsibilities

_____

_____

_____

_____

_____

▼

Putting the New Government to Work

_____

_____

_____

_____

Use after reading Chapter 10, pages 296–315.

NAME _____ DATE _____

BLAZING A TRAIL WEST

Identify Historical Figures

DIRECTIONS: On the blanks provided, write the word or name that best completes each sentence about Daniel Boone. Some letters in your answers will have numbers under them. Write these letters in the appropriate boxes below. You'll find the name of Daniel Boone's wife.

1. After the Revolutionary War, the land between the Appalachian Mountains and the

Mississippi River was called the American __ __ __ __ __ __ __ .
                                                                1

2. Settlers west of the Appalachians were called __ __ __ __ __ __ __ __ .
                                                                    12

3. Daniel Boone came to love the woods and hunting after his family moved to the

__ __ __ __ __ __   __ __ __ __ __ __ of North Carolina.
10   11

4. A man named __ __ __ __   __ __ __ __ __ __ told Boone stories
                                                        4
about land far to the west over the Appalachian Mountains.

5. After the French and Indian War, Boone set out to find an Indian trail called the

__ __ __ __ __ __ __ __ '   __ __ __ __ .
        9

6. Boone told about the rich land and buffalo in __ __ __ __ __ __ __ __ .
                                                                        6

7. Both the __ __ __ __ __ __ __ __ and Shawnees lived in settlements
              5   2
throughout this rich land.

8. Boone blazed a path through the Cumberland Gap that came to be known as the

__ __ __ __ __ __ __ __ __ __ __   __ __ __ __ .
                                                        7

9. Boone built a fort in this wilderness and named the new pioneer settlement

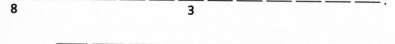
__ __ __ __ __ __ __ __ __ __ __ __ __ .
8   3

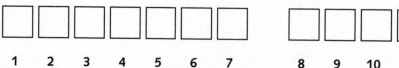

```
1   2   3   4   5   6   7      8   9   10  11  12
```

66 ACTIVITY BOOK   Use after reading Chapter 11, Lesson 1, pages 327–330.

Harcourt Brace School Publishers

Follow their Footsteps

Identify Historical Figures

DIRECTIONS: Each of the footprints below contains a paragraph that could have been written by one of the people involved with the Lewis and Clark expedition. Write the name of that person in the space provided.

One of my greatest accomplishments was the Louisiana Purchase. I asked the members of the Corps of Discovery to learn all they could about this new land.

_____
_____

As chief of the Shoshones, I welcomed the members of the Corps of Discovery. I was especially happy to see my sister. To help Lewis and Clark make their way over the Rockies, I gave them horses.

_____
_____

I was William Clark's slave. My skills in hunting and fishing made a valuable contribution to this exciting and informative expedition.

_____
_____

The leader of the expedition was my good friend. He chose me to go on the expedition because of my skills in cartography. We called our group of explorers the Corps of Discovery.

_____
_____

I was a Shoshone. The members of the expedition asked me to go with them to translate when they reached my tribe's lands. I agreed to go.

_____
_____

After working as an army officer in the wilderness of the Northwest Territory, I led the expedition to explore the lands of the Louisiana Purchase. I kept a journal of our experiences.

_____
_____

Harcourt Brace School Publishers

The Growth of NATIONALISM

Understand Cause and Effect

DIRECTIONS: Complete the following chart. Fill in either the cause or the effect.

CAUSES	EFFECTS
_____ _____	The Americans and the Indians fight the Battle of Tippecanoe.
_____ _____ _____ _____ _____	War fever pushes Congress to declare war on Britain in 1812.
American captain Oliver Hazard Perry defeats the British in a battle on Lake Erie on September 10, 1813.	_____ _____ _____
_____ _____	A wave of nationalism sweeps the country.
President Monroe wants to stop the growth of Spanish, French, and British colonies in the Americas.	_____ _____

Use after reading Chapter 11, Lesson 3, pages 336–340.

Harcourt Brace School Publishers

HOW TO PREDICT A LIKELY OUTCOME

Apply Thinking Skills

DIRECTIONS: The following flow chart lists the steps for predicting likely outcomes. Choose a school event, such as a test, that you expect to happen soon. Copy the flow chart onto another sheet of paper and use the steps to predict the outcome of the event.

THINK ABOUT WHAT YOU KNOW.

READ OR GATHER MORE INFORMATION.

MAKE A PREDICTION.

ASK YOURSELF SOME QUESTIONS:

Does the new information support my prediction?

Do I need to change my prediction?

DECIDE IF YOUR PREDICTION SEEMS CORRECT.

GO THROUGH THE STEPS AGAIN, IF NECESSARY.

The Flag
was still there

After the British attack on Fort McHenry, Francis Scott Key peered through the early dawn and saw that the American flag still flew over the fort. He wrote the words to "The Star-Spangled Banner," our national anthem, to honor this national symbol.

Understand Patriotic Symbols

DIRECTIONS: Read the statements below. Decide which statements tell how to respect and care for the flag and which statements give general information about the flag. Then place an X in the appropriate column.

	RESPECT/ CARE	GENERAL INFORMATION
1. The flag has 64 separate elements.		
2. The flag has the exact shades of blue and red, which are numbers 70075 and 70180 in the *Standard Color Card of America*.		
3. The flag is to be flown at half-mast as a mark of respect after the death of a major official.		
4. The present flag dates back to July 4, 1960, when the fiftieth star was added for Hawaii.		
5. The flag is taken down in bad weather.		
6. The flag is never to be allowed to touch anything beneath it, such as the ground, the floor, or water.		
7. The United States flag is called the "Stars and Stripes."		
8. The flag that Key wrote about had 15 stars and 15 stripes.		
9. Congress passed a law in 1818 requiring the flag to have 13 stripes to represent the original 13 colonies.		
10. The flag is to be displayed during school days in or near every school.		

Harcourt Brace School Publishers

Use after reading Chapter 11, Lesson 4, pages 342–345.

ON THE MOVE

Connect Main Ideas

DIRECTIONS: Use this organizer to show that you understand how the chapter's main ideas are connected. Complete the organizer by writing one or two sentences to tell about each person or pair of people or to summarize each event or idea.

On the Move

Across the Appalachians	The Louisiana Purchase	A Second War with Britain
Daniel Boone _____ _____ _____ _____ _____	The Purchase _____ _____ _____ _____ _____	Tecumseh and Tenskwatawa _____ _____ _____ _____ _____
Settling Kentucky _____ _____ _____ _____ _____	Lewis and Clark _____ _____ _____ _____ _____	War Fever _____ _____ _____ _____ _____
Pioneer Life _____ _____ _____ _____ _____	Zebulon Pike _____ _____ _____ _____ _____	The Era of Good Feelings _____ _____ _____ _____

Inventors
and their
Inventions

Link Past Technology to the Present

DIRECTIONS: Complete the following chart about inventions of the Industrial Revolution by filling in the missing information.

INVENTOR	INVENTION	IMPORTANCE OF INVENTION	WHAT YOUR LIFE WOULD BE LIKE WITHOUT THE INVENTION
Unknown	spinning machine		
Eli Whitney			
	one-factory system		
		speeded travel and trade over water	
	locomotive, the *Tom Thumb*		

Use after reading Chapter 12, Lesson 1, pages 349–354.

Harcourt Brace School Publishers

The Trail of Tears

Sequence Events

DIRECTIONS: Read the following events leading up to the Trail of Tears. Then identify the year in which each event took place. You may wish to review the information in your textbook before you begin.

_____ Gold is discovered on Cherokee lands; white settlers pour in to stake their claims.

_____ Chief Justice John Marshall gives the Court's ruling that the United States should protect the Cherokees and their lands in Georgia, but President Jackson ignores the ruling.

_____ Congress passes the Indian Removal Act, forcing all Indians living east of the Mississippi to move to Indian Territory in Oklahoma.

_____ The United States government agrees to accept the independence of the Cherokee nation.

_____ Andrew Jackson becomes the seventh President of the United States.

_____ Cherokees begin the journey that has come to be known as the Trail of Tears; more than 4,000 Cherokees die.

DIRECTIONS: Use the information above to complete the following activities.

1. Circle the date of the event that marks the beginning of forced relocation of native peoples from the East to the West.

2. Underline an economic reason why the Cherokees were forced from their lands.

3. Draw a box around the year that marks the beginning of the Trail of Tears.

4. On a separate sheet of paper, draw a horizontal time line using the dates and events listed above. Start your time line at 1790 and end it at 1840. Make one inch represent a ten-year period.

THE Oregon Trail

Arrange Information in Order

DIRECTIONS: Read the following sentences about a trip on the Oregon Trail. Then place the sentences in the proper order by numbering them from 1 to 6, with 1 being the earliest event and 6 being the latest event.

_____ A steamboat carries our family up the river to Independence, Missouri.

_____ The wagons arrive in Willamette Valley. Oregon at last!

_____ At nightfall the wagons circle for camp.

_____ We load our possessions onto the wagon and hear the cry, "Wagons roll!"

_____ We leave our home on the East Coast and board a train headed for St. Louis, Missouri.

_____ The sound of the bugle signals that breakfast is over, and we break camp.

DIRECTIONS: Study the list of supplies below. Then complete the activities that follow.

One box of sardines	$16	_____
One pound of hard bread	$ 2	_____
One pound of butter	$ 6	_____
One-half pound of cheese	$ 3	_____
Total		_____

1. Number the items from most expensive to least expensive in the spaces provided. Start numbering with *1* as the most expensive.

2. Write the total cost of the supplies in the space provided.

3. Imagine that you can spend $25. Put a line through the item or items that you would need to take off your list.

Use after reading Chapter 12, Lesson 3, pages 359–365.

NAME _____ DATE _____

HOW TO USE RELIEF and Elevation Maps

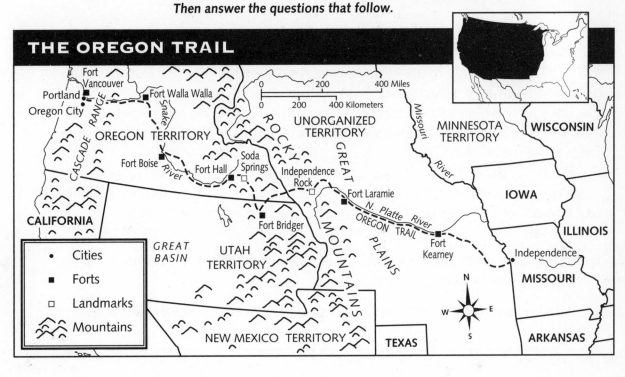

Map Skill · *Apply Map Skills*

DIRECTIONS: Study the map of the Oregon Trail. Then answer the questions that follow.

THE OREGON TRAIL

Fort Vancouver
Portland
Oregon City
Fort Walla Walla
CASCADE RANGE
OREGON TERRITORY
Snake River
Fort Boise
Fort Hall
Soda Springs
Independence Rock
ROCKY MOUNTAINS
GREAT PLAINS
UNORGANIZED TERRITORY
Missouri River
MINNESOTA TERRITORY
WISCONSIN
Fort Laramie
N. Platte River
OREGON TRAIL
Fort Kearney
IOWA
ILLINOIS
Independence
CALIFORNIA
GREAT BASIN
UTAH TERRITORY
Fort Bridger
MISSOURI
0   200   400 Miles
0   200   400 Kilometers
NEW MEXICO TERRITORY
TEXAS
ARKANSAS

Legend:
- • Cities
- ■ Forts
- □ Landmarks
- ⌃⌃ Mountains

1. Write in the correct sequence the names of the physical features you would pass through if you traveled the Oregon Trail from Independence, Missouri, to Fort Vancouver.

_____

_____

_____

2. Trace over the part of the Oregon Trail that passes through the Rocky Mountains.

Through which forts does this part of the trail pass? _____

3. Which river did the Oregon Trail follow just west of the Rocky Mountains?

_____

4. On a separate sheet of paper, describe the trip along the Oregon Trail from Independence to Portland. Include in your description the forts and landmarks along the way and the changes in the geography.

Seneca Falls

Compare Primary Sources

DIRECTIONS: Read the following opening lines of the Declaration of Sentiments. Complete the activities that follow by comparing these lines with the opening lines of the Declaration of Independence.

Declaration of Sentiments

When, in the course of human events, it becomes necessary for one portion of the family of man to assume among the people of the earth a position different from that which they have hitherto occupied, but one to which the laws of nature and of nature's God entitle them, a decent respect to the opinions of mankind requires that they should declare the causes that impel them to such a course.

We hold these truths to be self-evident: that all men and women are created equal; that they are endowed by their Creator with certain inalienable rights; that among these are life, liberty, and the pursuit of happiness. . . .

1. Underline the words in the Declaration of Sentiments that are different from the words in the Declaration of Independence.

2. Why do you think the writers of this document did not change the word "mankind"?

_____

_____

_____

3. Write the phrase from the Declaration of Independence that was completely left out of the Declaration of Sentiments. (Don't include words used as substitutes.)

_____

_____

_____

4. Why do you think the women at Seneca Falls would model the Declaration of Sentiments and Resolutions after the Declaration of Independence?

_____

_____

_____

Harcourt Brace School Publishers

NAME _____ DATE _____

HOW TO USE A
Double-Bar Graph

Apply Graph Skills

DIRECTIONS: Use the facts at the right to make a double-bar graph in the space below. Create a key and title for your graph. Then answer the questions on the next page.

POPULATION GROWTH 1790–1860 (IN THOUSANDS)		
YEAR	AFRICAN	WHITE
1790	757	3,172
1800	1,002	4,306
1810	1,378	5,862
1820	1,772	7,867
1830	2,329	10,537
1840	2,874	14,196
1850	3,639	19,553
1860	4,442	26,923

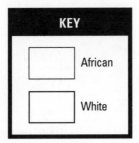

KEY

African

White

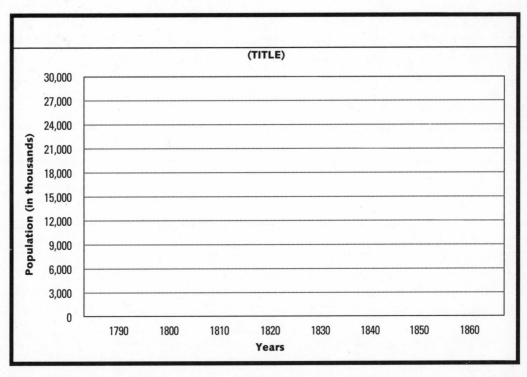

(TITLE)

Population (in thousands)

30,000
27,000
24,000
21,000
18,000
15,000
12,000
9,000
6,000
3,000
0

1790 1800 1810 1820 1830 1840 1850 1860

Years

Harcourt Brace School Publishers

(Continued)

NAME _____ DATE _____

1. What interval is used on the bar graph to show the increase in population?

   _____

2. What interval is used to show the passage of time? _____

3. How many years of data does this bar graph cover? _____

4. During which ten-year period did the white population grow the least?

   _____

5. During which 10-year period was there the least growth in the African population?

   _____

6. Compare the growth of the African population with that of the white population.
   List two generalizations you can make using the data.

   _____

   _____

   _____

   _____

   _____

   _____

7. Compare the table on page 77 with the double-bar graph you created. Which of the
   two makes it easier for you to understand the information? Why?

   _____

   _____

   _____

   _____

  Use after reading Chapter 12, Skill Lesson, page 373.

THE WAY WEST

Connect Main Ideas

DIRECTIONS: Use this organizer to show that you understand how the chapter's main ideas are connected. Complete the organizer by writing three supporting details for each main idea.

The Industrial Revolution
New technology changed life in the United States in the 1800s.

1. _____

2. _____

3. _____

The Age of Jackson
Americans in different parts of the country felt differently about concerns in the early 1800s.

1. _____

2. _____

3. _____

The Way West

N
W — E
S

Westward Ho!
The United States wanted its land to reach the Pacific Ocean.

1. _____

2. _____

3. _____

An Age of Reform
People in the 1800s worked to make American society better.

1. _____

2. _____

3. _____

A TALE OF TWO REGIONS
1860

Analyze Information in a Table

DIRECTIONS: The table below compares the North with the South in 1860. Use the information in your textbook to complete the table. Then answer the questions that follow to show you understand how the two regions differed.

TWO WAYS OF LIFE

	NORTH	SOUTH
Total Number of People		
Number of Enslaved People		
Number of Factories	119,500	20,850
Number of Factory Workers	1,300,000	110,000
Annual Value of Factory Products	$1,730,000,000	$156,000,000
Miles of Railroad Track	21,500	8,500
Value of Exports	$175,000,000	$226,000,000
Money in Banks	$345,900,000	$76,000,000

1. List three details from the table that support the idea that there was more manufacturing in the North than in the South.

_____

_____

_____

2. List one detail from the table that supports the idea that the South relied on trade with

other countries more than the North did. _____

_____

3. Which region had more miles of railroad track? _____
How might having more miles of railroad track affect that region's economy?

_____

_____

Use after reading Chapter 13, Lesson 1, pages 389–393.

Harcourt Brace School Publishers

HOW TO USE Graphs To Identify Trends

In the early 1800s most people in both the North and the South lived and worked on farms. Today, farming continues to be an important economic activity throughout much of the United States. However, the number of farms has changed greatly over time.

Apply Graph Skills

DIRECTIONS: *Use the facts at the right to make a line graph in the space below. Add a title to your graph. Then answer the questions that follow.*

Year	Number of Farms
1850	1,500,000
1880	4,000,000
1920	6,500,000
1980	2,400,000
1992	2,100,000

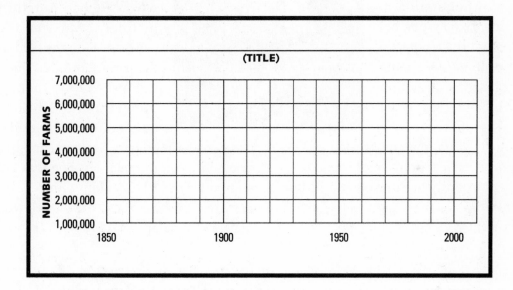

1. What was the trend between 1850 and 1920? _____

2. What was the trend between 1920 and 1992? _____

3. How would you explain the trends? _____

_____

_____

_____

THE LIFE AND TIMES OF A
SLAVE

Gather Information in Reference Books

DIRECTIONS: Read the passage from Frederick Douglass's autobiography, The Life and Times of Frederick Douglass.

My first experience of life, as I now remember it, began in the family of my grandmother and grandfather, Betsey and Isaac Bailey. . . .

. . . Whether because she [Grandmother Betsey] was too old for field service, or because she had so faithfully done the duties of her station in early life, I know not, but she enjoyed the special right of living in a cabin separate from the other cabins, having given her only the charge of the young children and the burden of her support. . . . The practice of separating mothers from their children and hiring them out at distances too great to allow their meeting, except after long periods of time, was a marked feature of the cruelty and hardness of the slave system. . . .

My grandmother's five daughters were hired out . . . and my only recollections of my own mother are of a few hasty visits made in the night on foot, after the daily tasks were over, and when she had to return in time to answer the driver's call to the field in the early morning. These glimpses of my mother under such conditions and against such odds, meager as they were, are permanently stamped upon my memory. She was tall and had dark, glossy skin with regular features, and amongst the slaves was remarkably sedate and dignified.

DIRECTIONS: Use the passage above and other available resources to answer the following questions about Frederick Douglass on a separate sheet of paper. For each question, tell whether you used only the passage to find the answer or whether you needed to use an encyclopedia, a dictionary, or some other reference book.

1. When was Frederick Douglass born, and when did he die?

2. In what state did Douglass live as a slave?

3. Who raised Douglass as a boy?

4. How did Douglass describe his mother?

Use after reading Chapter 13, Lesson 2, pages 395–399.

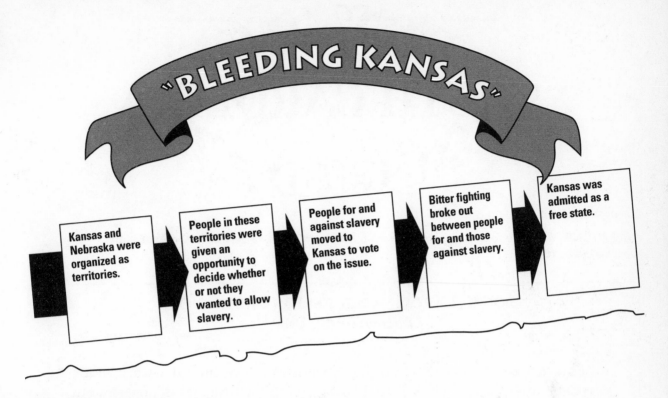

Expand Thinking About an Issue

**DIRECTIONS: Use the flow chart above and the information in
your textbook to answer the questions below.**

1. How did the Kansas–Nebraska Act deal with the spread of slavery?

_____

2. How do you think people in the North reacted to the Kansas–Nebraska Act?

_____

3. How do you think people in the South viewed the Kansas–Nebraska Act?

_____

4. What were the major effects of the Kansas–Nebraska Act in Kansas?

_____

5. Why did Southern states begin to talk more about secession after Kansas became a state?

_____

_____

6. Do you think the Kansas–Nebraska Act was a good law? Why or why not?

_____

WHY DID SOUTH CAROLINA SECEDE?

Recognize Point of View

DIRECTIONS: Read the following paragraph from the South Carolina Secession Ordinance of December 20, 1860.

SOUTH CAROLINA SECESSION ORDINANCE
December 20, 1860

An agreement between the states set up a government with specific purposes and powers. We feel that the reasons for which this government was begun have been defeated. The government itself has destroyed them by the action of the Northern, nonslaveholding states. **(1)** Those states have assumed the right to decide the properness of our domestic practices (that is, slavery). **(2)** They have denied our rights of property recognized by the Constitution. They have denounced as sinful the practice of slavery. **(3)** They have permitted the organization of abolitionist groups, whose goal is to disturb the peace of and to take away the property of the citizens of our states. **(4)** Those groups have encouraged and helped thousands of our slaves to leave their homes; and the slaves who remain have been incited by special agents, books, and pictures into insurrection.

DIRECTIONS: For each numbered sentence in the South Carolina Secession Ordinance, state in your own words a South Carolina complaint from a Southern point of view. Then respond with an appropriate explanation from a Northern point of view. Use your textbook if you need additional information.

Southern Complaint		Northern Response
1. _____		_____
2. _____		_____
3. _____		_____
4. _____		_____

Use after reading Chapter 13, Lesson 4, pages 405–408.

Harcourt Brace School Publishers

HOW TO MAKE A THOUGHTFUL DECISION

Apply Thinking Skills

DIRECTIONS: Think about a decision you made recently at school, or think about a decision that someone made during the Civil War. Then use the organizer below to record and analyze that decision. Fill in as many possible actions and consequences as you can.

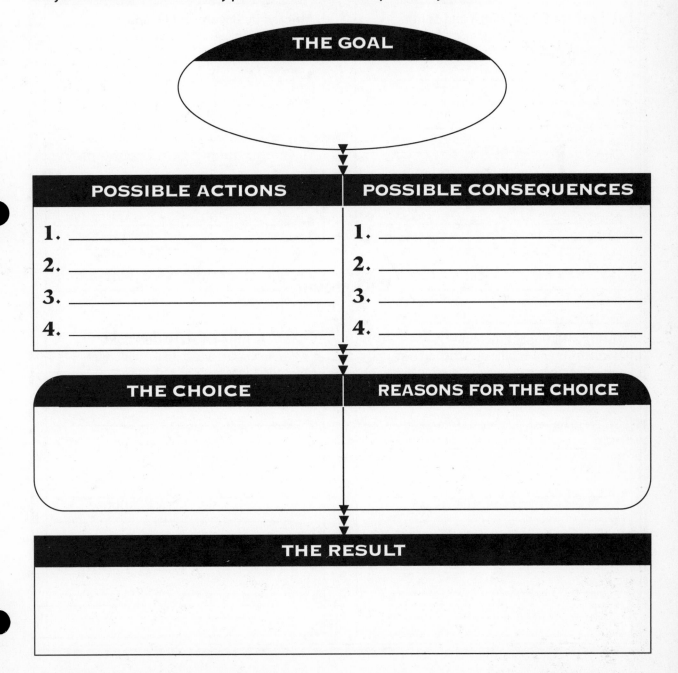

THE GOAL

POSSIBLE ACTIONS	POSSIBLE CONSEQUENCES
1. _____	1. _____
2. _____	2. _____
3. _____	3. _____
4. _____	4. _____

THE CHOICE | **REASONS FOR THE CHOICE**

THE RESULT

Harcourt Brace School Publishers

Background to the CONFLICT

Connect Main Ideas

DIRECTIONS: Use this organizer to show that you understand how the chapter's main ideas are connected. Complete the organizer by writing three details to support each main idea.

Differences Divide North and South
People in the North and the South disagreed during the mid-1800s.

1. _____
   _____
   _____

2. _____
   _____
   _____

3. _____
   _____
   _____

Africans in Slavery and Freedom
Enslaved people protested against being held in slavery.

1. _____
   _____
   _____

2. _____
   _____
   _____

3. _____
   _____
   _____

Background to the Conflict

Facing a National Problem
Northerners and Southerners tried to settle disagreements during the early 1800s.

1. _____
   _____
   _____

2. _____
   _____
   _____

3. _____
   _____
   _____

A Time for Hard Decisions
Americans had to make important decisions in 1860 and 1861.

1. _____
   _____
   _____

2. _____
   _____
   _____

3. _____
   _____
   _____

Use after reading Chapter 13, pages 388–413.

THE BONNIE BLUE FLAG

When South Carolina joined the Confederacy, its flag changed, but Harry Macarthy's song, "The Bonnie Blue Flag," which was about South Carolina's first flag, quickly became the Confederacy's national anthem.

Link Music to History

DIRECTIONS: Read the words to the song. Then answer the questions that follow.

Verse One
1. We are a band of brothers, and native to the soil,
2. Fighting for the property we gained by honest toil;
3. And when our rights were threatened, the cry rose near and far:
4. Hurrah! for the bonnie blue flag that bears a single star.

Verse Two
1. As long as the Union was faithful to her trust,
2. Like friends and like brothers, kind were we and just;
3. But now, when Northern treachery attempts our rights to mar,
4. We hoist, on high, the bonnie blue flag that bears a single star.

Last Verse
1. Then here's to our Confederacy—strong we are and brave,
2. Like patriots of old, we'll fight, our heritage to save;
3. And rather than submit to shame, to die we would prefer—
4. So cheer for the bonnie blue flag that bears a single star.

Chorus
1. Hurrah! hurrah! for Southern rights! hurrah!
2. Hurrah! for the bonnie blue flag that bears a single star.

1. Name two things that are repeated in line 4 of each verse.

_____

2. Which line in Verse One describes how the Confederate soldiers felt about one another?

Describe that feeling. _____

_____

3. Each verse has one line that states a reason that the Confederacy was fighting. List each line number and give the reason.

Verse One   Line Number: _____   Reason: _____

Verse Two   Line Number: _____   Reason: _____

Last Verse   Line Number: _____   Reason: _____

Harcourt Brace School Publishers

Use after reading Chapter 14, Lesson 1, pages 415–419.

NAME _____ DATE _____

THE *Emancipation Proclamation*

Interpret Primary Source Documents

DIRECTIONS: The passage below from the Emancipation Proclamation contains words in boldface type. Use context clues to define those words. Match each word in the list with its definition, and write the correct letter in the blank. Then, on a separate sheet of paper, answer the questions that follow.

And by **virtue** of the power and for the purpose **aforesaid,** I do order and declare that all persons held as slaves within said **designated** States and parts of States are, and **henceforward** shall be, free; and that the Executive Government of the United States, including the military and naval authorities thereof, will recognize and maintain the freedom of said persons.

And I hereby enjoin upon the people so declared to be free to **abstain** from all violence, unless in necessary self-defense; and I recommend to them that, in all cases when allowed, they labor faithfully for reasonable wages.

And I further declare and make known that such persons of **suitable** condition will be received into the armed service of the United States to **garrison** forts, positions, stations, and other places, and to **man** vessels of all sorts in said service.

_____ virtue   **A.** pointed out; shown

_____ aforesaid   **B.** from this time on

_____ designated   **C.** because of; on the grounds of

_____ henceforward   **D.** right; proper

_____ abstain   **E.** spoken of before; mentioned previously

_____ suitable   **F.** to station troops in a fort or town

_____ garrison   **G.** to take an assigned place for work or defense

_____ man   **H.** to keep oneself back; to choose not to do

1. What is the most important message in the first paragraph?

2. What did President Lincoln recommend to former slaves in the second paragraph?

3. In the last paragraph, what did President Lincoln declare about the armed services?

Use after reading Chapter 14, Lesson 2, pages 420–424.

★ CIVIL WAR ★

HORSES

Apply Information from a Chart

DIRECTIONS: Study the chart below. Then complete the activities that follow.

	CIVIL WAR GENERALS' HORSES			
HORSE'S NAME	**RIDER'S NAME**	**ARMY**	**DESCRIPTION**	**FURTHERMORE**
Don Juan	George Armstrong Custer	Union	Bay stallion	Custer had more horses (7) killed under him than any other Union leader.
Butler	Wade Hampton	Confederate	Bay stallion	One of Hampton's officers gave him the horse as a gift.
Sam	William Tecumseh Sherman	Union	Half-breed bay stallion	The horse was so steady under gunfire that Sherman could write orders while riding.
Lexington	William Tecumseh Sherman	Union	Kentucky thoroughbred	Sherman rode Lexington during his final review of his army.
Traveller	Robert E. Lee	Confederate	Iron gray gelding	Traveller was called the greatest warhorse of all time, except for Alexander the Great's horse.
Old Spot	Judson Kilpatrick	Union	Arabian	The horse outlived his master.

1. Underline the name of the general who had seven horses killed under him.

2. Put a star next to the name of each general who rode a bay stallion.

3. Put a box around the name of the horse that outlived his master.

4. a) Imagine you are a Civil War general. Explain why it is important to choose a good horse.

_____

_____

_____

b) Which of the horses on the chart would you have chosen? Explain your answer.

_____

_____

NAME _____ DATE _____

HOW TO COMPARE MAPS with DIFFERENT SCALES

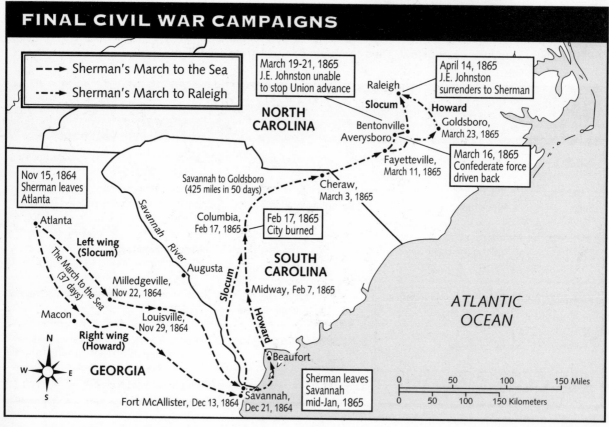

FINAL CIVIL WAR CAMPAIGNS

- – – → Sherman's March to the Sea
- –·–·→ Sherman's March to Raleigh

March 19-21, 1865
J.E. Johnston unable
to stop Union advance

April 14, 1865
J.E. Johnston
surrenders to Sherman

Raleigh

NORTH CAROLINA

Slocum   Howard

Bentonville   Goldsboro,
Averysboro   March 23, 1865

Fayetteville,
March 11, 1865

March 16, 1865
Confederate force
driven back

Nov 15, 1864
Sherman leaves
Atlanta

Savannah to Goldsboro
(425 miles in 50 days)

Cheraw,
March 3, 1865

Atlanta

Columbia,
Feb 17, 1865

Feb 17, 1865
City burned

**Left wing
(Slocum)**

Savannah River

Augusta

SOUTH CAROLINA

The March to the Sea
(37 days)

Milledgeville,
Nov 22, 1864

Midway, Feb 7, 1865

Macon

Slocum

ATLANTIC OCEAN

Louisville,
Nov 29, 1864

Howard

**Right wing
(Howard)**

GEORGIA

Beaufort

N
W E
S

Fort McAllister, Dec 13, 1864

Savannah,
Dec 21, 1864

Sherman leaves
Savannah
mid-Jan, 1865

0   50   100   150 Miles

0   50   100   150 Kilometers

Apply Map Skills

DIRECTIONS: Compare the map above with the map in your textbook on page 429.
*For each of the following statements, decide which map is more useful. Write A in the
answer blank if the map above is better and B if the textbook map is better.*

_____ **1.** Show the most miles per inch.

_____ **2.** Determine the distance between
Cheraw and Fayetteville.

_____ **3.** Determine how many miles
Sherman traveled on his March
to the Sea.

_____ **4.** Identify the extent of the
Union blockade.

_____ **5.** Measure the distance from
Atlanta, Georgia to
Macon, Georgia.

_____ **6.** Identify battles that took place
in Mississippi and Virginia.

_____ **7.** Determine the number of miles
traveled by Sherman's army
between February 17, 1865 and
March 11, 1865.

Use after reading Chapter 14, Skill Lesson, pages 432–433.

IT'S IN THE BAG!

Interpret Visuals and Point of View

DIRECTIONS: Study the illustrations and the captions below. Then on a separate sheet of paper, answer the questions that follow.

After the Civil War, inexpensive suitcases called carpetbags (above) were made from carpeting.

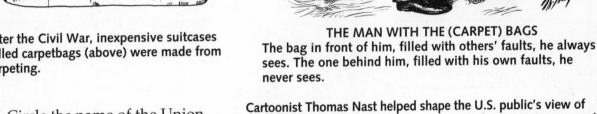

THE MAN WITH THE (CARPET) BAGS
The bag in front of him, filled with others' faults, he always sees. The one behind him, filled with his own faults, he never sees.

Cartoonist Thomas Nast helped shape the U.S. public's view of Reconstruction. This 1872 cartoon shows a former Union general.

1. Circle the name of the Union general in Nast's cartoon.

2. Underline the direction in which the general is heading.

3. Compare the bags in the cartoon with the one in the illustration next to the cartoon. What similarities and differences do you notice?

4. Look at the illustration on the left. How do you think this type of bag got its name?

5. How do you think Nast viewed the type of person in this cartoon? List the features of this cartoon that support your answer.

6. Nast said about this cartoon, "The bag in front of him filled with others' faults, he always sees. The one behind him, filled with his own faults, he never sees." Explain what you think Nast meant.

Use after reading Chapter 14, Lesson 4, pages 434–439.

Civil War and Reconstruction

Connect Main Ideas

DIRECTIONS: Use this organizer to show that you understand how the chapter's main ideas are connected. Complete the organizer by writing sentences to support the main ideas.

Choosing Sides

1. Most Northerners _____

_____

_____

2. Most Southerners _____

_____

_____

3. Other people _____

_____

_____

Vicksburg

_____

_____

_____

_____

Plans for Rebuilding

1. President Johnson _____

_____

_____

_____

Civil War

and

Reconstruction

Battle Plans

1. The North _____

_____

_____

_____

2. The South _____

_____

_____

The Emancipation Proclamation

_____

_____

_____

The March to the Sea

_____

_____

_____

_____

Plans for Rebuilding

2. Congress _____

_____

_____

_____

Use after reading Chapter 14, pages 414–441.

Famous Entrepreneurs

Categorize Information

DIRECTIONS: Read the stories that follow, and use the information to fill in the chart. Use your textbook and library reference materials to fill in the information about Andrew Carnegie.

Levi Strauss, a Jewish immigrant from Germany, left New York City for the West in 1850. He went west to sell canvas to settlers to use for sails and coverings for their wagons. When he arrived there, he found that settlers could not find pants strong enough to last. Strauss took his canvas material and made it into the first pair of jeans. His company became Levi Strauss & Co.

John Harvey Kellogg, of British ancestry, believed that a healthful diet would help people heal more quickly from illness. He was once sued by an elderly woman who broke her false teeth on a zwieback (hard bread) that he had recommended for her to eat. As a result of this incident, he started to think about producing a softer ready-to-eat food. One night he dreamed of how to make flaked foods. This dream resulted in his producing the first dry cereal, which today is known as Kellogg's Corn Flakes.

Fannie Merritt Farmer was born in Boston of British descent. She suffered a childhood illness that left her with a limp. After doctors discouraged her from going to college, she entered cooking school in 1887. By 1891 she was running it! In those days, cooking ingredients were measured by "pinches and dabs." Farmer applied science to cooking. In her best-selling cookbook, she standardized measurements. You can thank her for the level teaspoon.

FAMOUS ENTREPRENEURS			
ENTREPRENEUR	HERITAGE	COMPANY/PRODUCT	FUN FACT
Levi Strauss			
John Harvey Kellogg			
Fannie Merritt Farmer			
Andrew Carnegie			

Use after reading Chapter 15, Lesson 1, pages 453–457.

NAME _____ DATE _____

HOW TO USE A Time Zone MAP

Apply Map Skills

DIRECTIONS: Study the time zone map below. The clock in the eastern time zone is set at 11:00 A.M. Draw the hands on the clocks in the other time zones, and note whether the time shown is A.M. or P.M. Then use different colors to shade in the time zones on the map and the key.

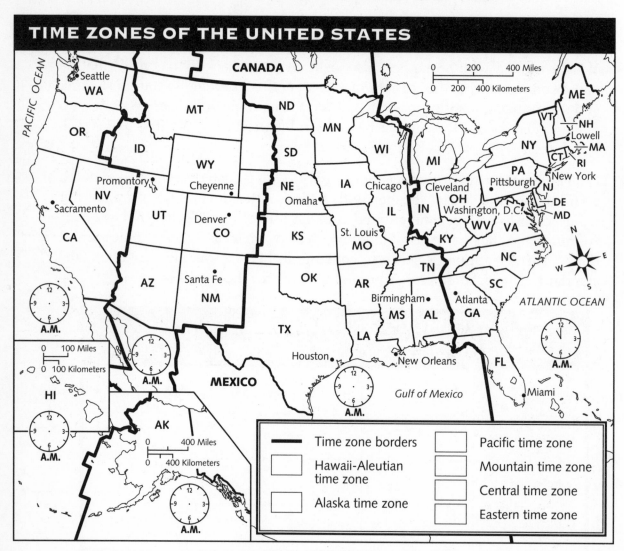

TIME ZONES OF THE UNITED STATES

Time zone borders
Hawaii-Aleutian time zone
Alaska time zone
Pacific time zone
Mountain time zone
Central time zone
Eastern time zone

(Continued)

Harcourt Brace School Publishers

Use after reading Chapter 15, Skill Lesson, pages 458–459.

DIRECTIONS: Study the time zone map on page 94. Complete the activities that follow.

1. How many time zones are located in the United States? _____

2. In which time zone is your city located? _____

3. In which time zones are the following cities located:

   Chicago, Illinois _____   St. Louis, Missouri _____

   Cleveland, Ohio _____   Atlanta, Georgia _____

4. Andrew Carnegie produced his steel in Pittsburgh, Pennsylvania. If he transported it by railroad from Pittsburgh to the West Coast, through how many time zones would

   the steel travel? _____

5. John D. Rockefeller set up an oil refinery in Cleveland, Ohio. He later bought refineries in West Virginia. If he traveled from his refinery in Ohio to his refinery in West Virginia,

   through how many time zones would he travel? _____

   _____

6. The Union Pacific Railroad built west from Omaha, Nebraska. The Central Pacific Railroad built east from Sacramento, California.

   a) If it is 7:00 P.M. in Sacramento, what time is it in Omaha? _____

   b) If it is 8:00 A.M. in Omaha, what time is it in Sacramento? _____

7. The two railroads met at Promontory, Utah. If it is 10 A.M. in Promontory,

   a) What time is it in Omaha? _____

   b) What time is it in Sacramento? _____

8. If the Super Bowl aired on TV from New Orleans at 3:00 P.M., what time would sports fans

   in Hawaii have to turn on their television sets to see the game? _____

9. Imagine you live in Denver, Colorado, and have a scheduled school lunch at noon.

   a) What time would it be in our nation's capital? _____

   b) What do you think students in the nation's capital would be doing at that time?

   _____

   _____

ORGANIZING
Resources

Understand Economics

DIRECTIONS: Three kinds of resources are needed to make a product: natural resources, or raw materials, such as minerals and ores; capital resources, such as money, tools, and equipment; and human resources, or workers. Conduct library research and complete the organizer below to show what resources are needed to make each product listed in the center box.

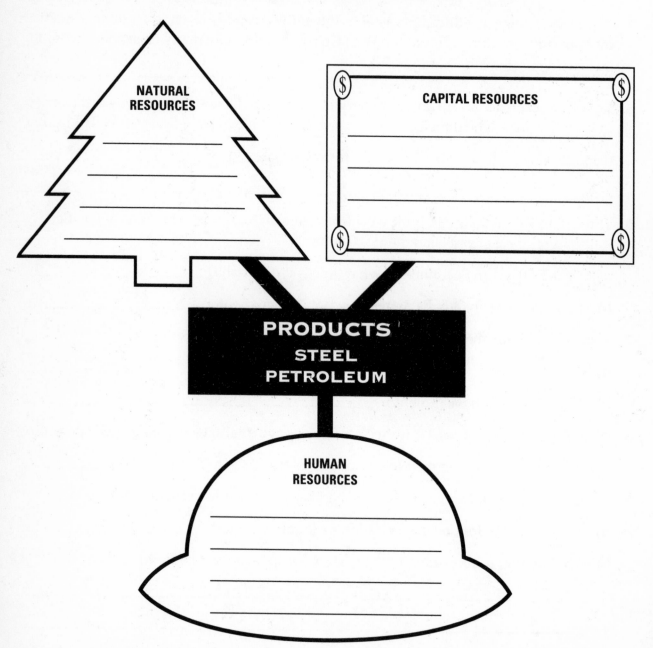

NATURAL
RESOURCES

CAPITAL RESOURCES

PRODUCTS
STEEL
PETROLEUM

HUMAN
RESOURCES

Harcourt Brace School Publishers

Use after reading Chapter 15, Lesson 2, pages 460–464.

Immigration

Distinguish Fact from Opinion

DIRECTIONS: Study the quotations below, which were made by immigrants who came to the United States at the beginning of the twentieth century. Then decide which of the following statements is fact and which is opinion. Write an F next to the statements of fact. Write an O next to the statements of opinion.

As far as Ellis Island was concerned, it was a nightmare. After all, none of us spoke English.

Nina Goodenov

The examiner [at Ellis Island] sat bureaucratically . . . I was questioned as to the state of my finances and I produced the required twenty-five dollars.

Louis Adamic

We lived there [Ellis Island] for three days . . . Because of the rigorous physical examination that we had to submit to, particularly of the eyes, there was this terrible anxiety that one of us might be rejected.

Angelo Pellegrini

America is . . . the great Melting Pot where all the races of Europe are melting and re-forming.

Israel Zangwill

_____ **1.** Ellis Island was a nightmare.

_____ **2.** Immigrants were required to produce $25 to enter the United States.

_____ **3.** Immigrants had to take a physical examination.

_____ **4.** The examiner at Ellis Island was unfriendly.

_____ **5.** America is a great Melting Pot.

_____ **6.** Immigrants who were not in good physical health could be rejected from the United States.

_____ **7.** Some immigrants had to spend several days waiting on Ellis Island.

_____ **8.** Many immigrants could not speak English.

AN African American PORTRAIT

Read a Table

DIRECTIONS: Study this table, which shows what percentage of the African American population lived in different regions of the United States during different time periods. Look for patterns. Then complete the activities that follow.

AFRICAN AMERICANS IN THE UNITED STATES, BY REGION (in percentages)

YEAR	NORTHEAST	NORTH CENTRAL	SOUTH	WEST
1860	3.5	4.1	92.2	0.1
1870	3.7	5.6	90.6	0.1
1880	3.5	5.9	90.5	0.2
1890	3.6	5.8	90.3	0.4
1900	4.4	5.6	89.7	0.3
1910	4.9	5.5	89.0	0.5
1920	6.5	7.6	85.2	0.8
1930	9.6	10.6	78.7	1.0

1. In which region did the percentage of African Americans decrease steadily from

1860 to 1930? _____

2. In which region did the percentage of African Americans increase the most from 1860 to 1930? What was the amount of percentage increase in this region?

_____

3. During which ten-year period did the percentage of African Americans living in the South decrease the most? How much of a decrease was there during this period?

_____

4. Migration was one reason that the percentage of African Americans in the South decreased during this time. Reread Jacob Lawrence's *The Great Migration: An American Story* in your textbook. Look for reasons that African Americans migrated. Copy the following headings onto a separate sheet of paper, and use information from the story to complete a chart showing reasons for African American migration.

FACTORS PUSHING AFRICAN AMERICANS OUT OF THE SOUTH	FACTORS PULLING AFRICAN AMERICANS TO OTHER REGIONS

Use after reading Chapter 15, Lesson 4, pages 470–474.

School Days

Relate Past to Present

DIRECTIONS: The following excerpt from Immigrant Kids by Russell Freedman describes a typical school day in New York City in the early 1900s. Read the excerpt. Then answer the questions that follow.

When teacher called out in her sharp, penetrating voice, "Class!" everyone sat up straight as a ramrod, eyes front, hands clasped rigidly behind one's back. We strived painfully to please her. With a thin smile of approval on her face, her eyes roved over the stiff, rigid figures in front of her.

Beautiful script letters across the huge blackboard and a chart of the alphabet were the sole adornments of the classroom. Every day the current lesson from our speller was meticulously written out on the blackboard by the teacher. . . . We spent hours over our copybooks, all conveniently lined, as we laboriously sought to imitate this perfection.

We had to learn our lessons by heart, and we repeated them out loud until we memorized them. Playgrounds were nonexistent, toilets were in the yard, and gymnasiums were an unheard-of luxury.

1. Use context clues to define *penetrating*. _____

2. Use context clues to describe your image of a ramrod. _____

_____

_____

3. Compare the adornments, or decorations, in the classroom described with the ones in

your classroom. _____

_____

4. Describe differences between the way the teacher presented lessons in the early 1900s and the way your teacher presents lessons. Include descriptions of methods and materials.

_____

_____

5. On a separate sheet of paper, write three paragraphs about your school, using the above three paragraphs as a guide. Describe the same things described in each paragraph, but use your school and class as the topic.

Harcourt Brace School Publishers

NAME ______________________ DATE ____________

HOW TO SOLVE A PROBLEM

Apply Thinking Skills

DIRECTIONS: Choose a problem in your school, such as those related to school lunches, bus schedules, or class size. Use the flow chart below to suggest a solution. You may copy the flow chart onto a separate sheet of paper if necessary.

Decide what the problem is. List the problem.

____

____

Think of possible solutions. List the solutions.

____

____

Think about the possible results of each solution. List the possible results of each solution.

____

____

Choose one solution. List this solution.

____

____

Think about how well your solution solves the problem. Explain how your solution solves the problem.

____

____

Use after reading Chapter 15, Skill Lesson, page 479.

INDUSTRY AND IMMIGRATION

Connect Main Ideas

DIRECTIONS: Use this organizer to show that you understand how the chapter's main ideas are connected. Complete the organizer by writing three examples to support each main idea.

New inventions changed life in the United States

1. _____
_____

2. _____
_____

3. _____
_____

Industry and Immigration

People faced problems as cities grew larger, and they worked to solve them.

1. _____
_____

2. _____
_____

3. _____
_____

People fought for better working conditions.

1. _____
_____

2. _____
_____

3. _____
_____

Immigrants in the United States faced problems.

1. _____
_____

2. _____
_____

3. _____
_____

African Americans shared problems with other new-comers to cities.

1. _____
_____

2. _____
_____

3. _____
_____

Use after reading Chapter 15, pages 452–481.

Life in a Sod House

Illustrate History

DIRECTIONS: The following excerpt is from Frontier Living by Edwin Tunis. Read the excerpt. Then complete the activities that follow.

A family couldn't live forever in its wagon and the Homestead Act required a house; but there wasn't enough wood for a house. The Mandan and the Pawnee Indians solved the problem with earth lodges and the white men did the same; they cut the sod into blocks and laid up walls with it as bricks are laid. . . . If they could find a bank, they dug the back of the house into it, building only the front and part of the side walls of sod. Poles for roof rafters came from a river bank and on them the builders spread brush, grass, and more sod. The floor was dirt. Canvas or leather made a door, and anything but glass covered a window. A ditch across the bank behind the dugout and down the slope on either side prevented a complete washout, but the roofs of dugouts and of four-walled "soddies," too, leaked so badly that people customarily hung small tents over their beds. Even in dry weather, dirt falling from the roof got over and into everything; women loathed [hated] the soddies. Dirt wasn't all that fell; there were also bugs and mice and sometimes a cow wandered onto a dugout roof and suddenly joined the family below.

1. Why did the homesteaders build sod houses?

_____

2. List the steps homesteaders followed to build sod houses.

_____

_____

3. On a separate sheet of paper, describe what it was like to live in a sod house, and explain how you would feel if you had to live in such a house.

4. Use the above description of life in a sod house to draw a diagram of a sod house. Make sure you label each part of the house.

Harcourt Brace School Publishers

Use after reading Chapter 16, Lesson 1, pages 483–487.

HOW TO READ A Climograph

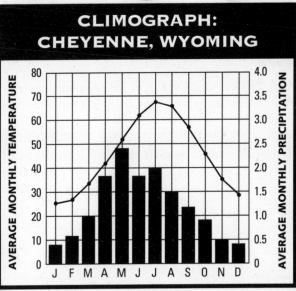

CLIMOGRAPH: CHEYENNE, WYOMING

Apply Graph Skills

DIRECTIONS: *Below is a table that provides average monthly temperature and precipitation data for Pittsburgh, Pennsylvania. Answer the questions that follow by comparing the data in this table with the climograph of Cheyenne, Wyoming, at the right.*

Temperature is given in degrees Fahrenheit. Precipitation is given in inches.

KEY

• Temperature ■ Precipitation

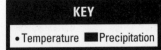

PITTSBURGH, PENNSYLVANIA												
	Jan	Feb	Mar	April	May	June	July	Aug	Sept	Oct	Nov	Dec
Temperature	30	31	40	51	62	71	75	73	67	55	43	34
Precipitation	2.9	2.5	3.3	3.1	3.3	3.7	4.0	3.2	2.7	2.5	2.4	2.7

1. During which month does Cheyenne receive the most precipitation?

_____ Pittsburgh? _____

2. Which place is more likely to require irrigation for farming? _____

Why? _____

3. Using precipitation as a guide, list what type of climate you think each city might

have. Explain your choice. _____

_____

4. Which place has the warmer summer? _____

Which place has the colder winter? _____

5. Use the physical map in the atlas of your textbook to explain why one place is colder

on average than the other. _____

_____

Use after reading Chapter 16, Skill Lesson, pages 488–489.

NAME ______________________________ DATE ____________

World Roundup

Read a Table

DIRECTIONS: Study the chart below, which describes cowhands from around the world. Then complete the activities that follow.

NAME	LOCATION	CLOTHING	MISCELLANEOUS FACTS
cowhand	United States	chaps, brimmed hat, spurs, cotton shirt, bandanna, boots, blue jeans, holster	most famous in world because of legendary role on the western frontier
gardian	France	flat-crowned, wide-brimmed black hat; brightly colored shirt; black velvet jacket; heavy cotton trousers	herded special black bulls raised just for bullfights; rode white horses
gaucho	Argentina and Uruguay	bloused trousers called *bombachas;* tall, small-brimmed hat; knotted scarf	word *gaucho* comes from South American Indian word for "outcast"
vaquero	Mexico	wide-brimmed, felt sombrero or straw hat; cloak or plain, short jacket; flared woolen trousers or cotton pants.	owned no land and often no horse; rode horses belonging to others; taught American cowhands their trade

1. Circle the name of the cowhand that is located in Europe.
2. Put a star next to the name of the cowhand that is located in South America.
3. Put an **X** next to the names of the cowhands that are located in North America.
4. Choose the cowhand from the chart that you find the most interesting. Use the information in the chart to draw a diagram of what you think your selected cowhand looks like. Be sure to label your diagram and include a caption describing why you think this cowhand is the most interesting.

Use after reading Chapter 16, Lesson 2, pages 490–494.

THE STAGECOACH RIDE WEST

Describe a Method of Transportation

DIRECTIONS: Study the diagram of a stagecoach. Answer the questions. Then, on a separate sheet of paper, complete the writing assignment.

STAGECOACH

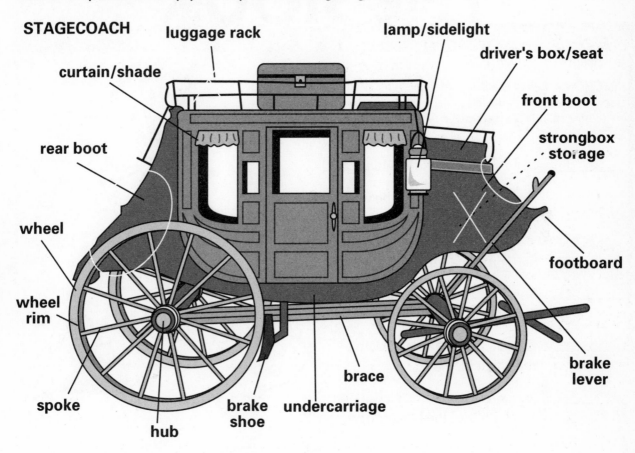

luggage rack
lamp/sidelight
driver's box/seat
curtain/shade
front boot
rear boot
strongbox storage
wheel
footboard
wheel rim
brake lever
brace
spoke
brake shoe
undercarriage
hub

1. A boot is a trunk or baggage compartment. Circle the two boots on the stagecoach.

2. Put an **X** through two other places on the stagecoach made specifically for storage.

3. How do you think a stagecoach was powered? _____

4. Stagecoach roads were extremely bumpy because of the drainage ditches that cut across them. When the roads ended, the ride continued on an even rougher trail. Study the physical map in the atlas in your textbook. Imagine that you are traveling by stagecoach from the Missouri River to the Rocky Mountains. The trip will take six days. Write a journal account of your trip describing the scenery and your feelings about the trip.

Harcourt Brace School Publishers

THE UNITED STATES & THE SIOUX

Put Events in Sequence

DIRECTIONS: Below is a listing of nine events discussed in the lesson. In the blank to the left of each event, place a number from one to nine to indicate the order in which these events took place.

_____ Gold discovered in the Black Hills.

_____ Railroads built across the Great Plains.

_____ U.S. soldiers march into Black Hills area.

_____ Sioux returned to their reservation.

_____ Sioux refuse United States offer to purchase Black Hills area.

_____ Fifteen million buffalo roam the Great Plains.

_____ Sioux reservation created in the Black Hills of the Dakota Territory.

_____ George Custer and his troops killed at the Battle of Little Bighorn.

_____ Fewer than one thousand buffalo roam the Great Plains.

DIRECTIONS: Listed below are five names. Circle the one name that does not belong, and explain why.

Geronimo   Joseph   Crazy Horse   Custer   Sitting Bull

_____

_____

Use after reading Chapter 16, Lesson 4, pages 498–501.

THE LAST FRONTIER

Connect Main Ideas

DIRECTIONS: *Use this organizer to show that you understand how the chapter's main ideas are connected. Complete the organizer by writing two or three sentences that summarize the main idea of each lesson.*

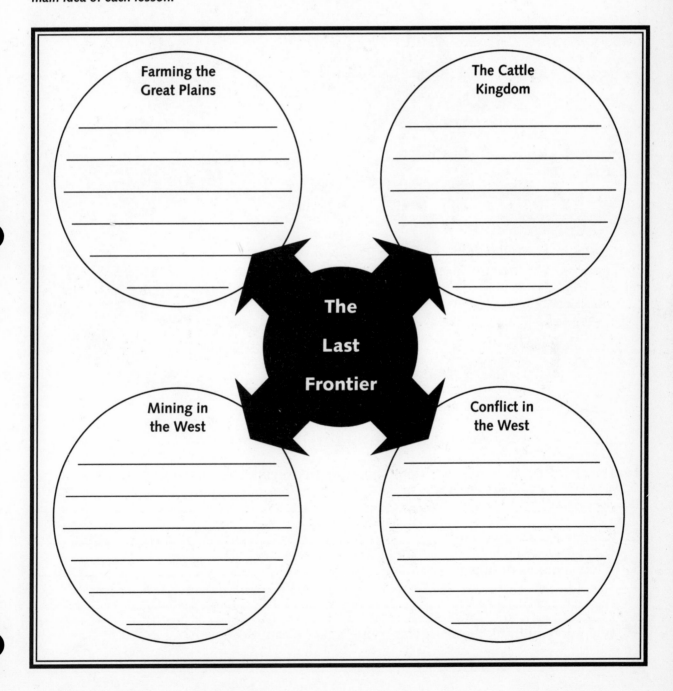

Farming the Great Plains

The Cattle Kingdom

The Last Frontier

Mining in the West

Conflict in the West

Use after reading Chapter 16, pages 482–503.

The Big-Stick Policy

Interpret a Political Cartoon

DIRECTIONS: Study the political cartoon. Then answer the questions that follow.

THE BIG STICK IN THE CARIBBEAN SEA

1. The character shown is President Theodore Roosevelt. Describe his appearance.

_____

2. What is Roosevelt doing? _____

3. What symbols of power are shown with Roosevelt? _____

_____

4. What do you think the artist was trying to say about Roosevelt?

_____

Harcourt Brace School Publishers

HOW TO COMPARE MAP Projections

Only a globe can show exact shape, size, direction, and distance on the Earth. Cartographers try to show these four features of the Earth on a flat map as exactly as possible, but all map projections have distortions.

Apply Map Skills

DIRECTIONS: *Study the map projections on this page and the following page. Then read each statement on the next page. Decide whether the statement applies to a Mercator projection, to a Mollweide projection, or to both projections. Place a check on the correct line or lines.*

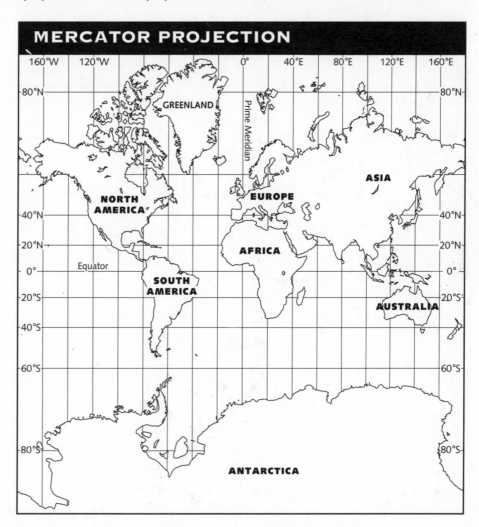

(Continued)

NAME _____ DATE _____

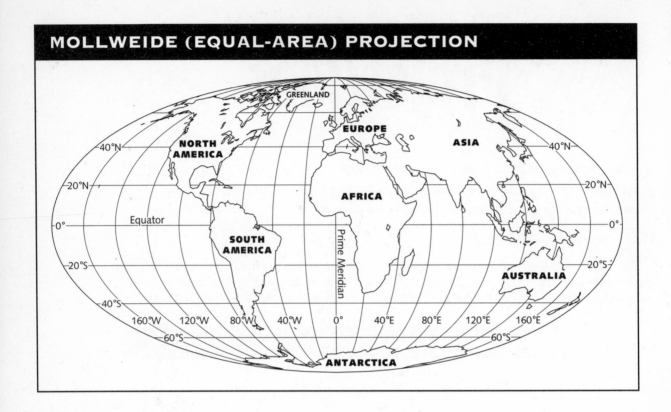

MOLLWEIDE (EQUAL-AREA) PROJECTION

Mercator   **Mollweide**

_____ _____ **1.** Shows the seven continents.

_____ _____ **2.** Shows the curved feature of the Earth.

_____ _____ **3.** Uses straight lines for all lines of latitude and longitude.

_____ _____ **4.** Shows all lines of latitude and longitude at right angles to each other.

_____ _____ **5.** Uses a straight line for the equator.

_____ _____ **6.** Uses a straight line for the prime meridian.

_____ _____ **7.** Shows meridians intersecting at the top and bottom of the map.

_____ _____ **8.** Shows parallels NOT intersecting.

_____ _____ **9.** Uses straight lines to show compass directions.

_____ _____ **10.** Shows sizes of places true to scale.

_____ _____ **11.** Shows Greenland as about the same size as Africa.

_____ _____ **12.** Shows exact distances more accurately.

Use after reading Chapter 17, Skill Lesson, pages 522–523.

NAME _____ DATE _____

Which Progressive SAID THAT?

Identify Progressives and Their Reforms

DIRECTIONS: The statements that follow express the ideas of Theodore Roosevelt, Robert La Follette, and W. E. B. Du Bois. Write TR next to statements that could have been made by Theodore Roosevelt, LF next to those that could have been made by La Follette, and DB next to those that could have been made by Du Bois.

_____ **1.** My reform program was called the Wisconsin Idea.

_____ **2.** My reform program was called the Square Deal.

_____ **3.** I helped start the National Association for the Advancement of Colored People (NAACP).

_____ **4.** I encouraged Congress to pass the Pure Food and Drug Act and the Meat Inspection Act.

_____ **5.** I set up the merit system to make sure people were qualified for government jobs.

_____ **6.** I wanted African Americans to be proud of their heritage and culture.

_____ **7.** With my help, my state legislature passed a law listing jobs for which children could not be hired.

_____ **8.** I worked to change laws that did not give full civil rights to African Americans.

_____ **9.** I had land in many parts of the country set aside for wilderness areas and national parks.

_____ **10.** I encouraged the passage of a law limiting the workday to no more than ten hours.

Harcourt Brace School Publishers

OVER THERE

Understand Patriotic Songs

DIRECTIONS: George M. Cohan's song "Over There" served as the American theme song for World War I. Study the song's words, and complete the activities that follow.

Hear them calling you and me;
Ev'ry son of liberty.
Hurry right away, no delay, go today,
Make your daddy glad, to have had such a lad,
Tell your sweetheart not to pine,
To be proud her boy's in line.

> CHORUS:
> Over there, over there,
> Send the word, send the word over there,
> That the Yanks are coming,
> The Yanks are coming,
> The drums rum-tumming ev'ry where—
> So prepare, say a pray'r,
> Send the word, send the word to beware,
> We'll be over, we're coming over,
> And we won't come back till it's over over there.

Hoist the flag and let her fly,
Like true heroes, do or die.
Pack your little kit, show your grit, do your bit,
Soldiers to the ranks from the towns and the tanks,
Make your mother proud of you,
And to liberty be true.

1. Underline the people in the song whom the soldiers are going to make proud.

2. In the first line of the first verse, who does "them" refer to? _____

3. Reread the chorus. Who are the Yanks? _____

Who needs to beware of the Yanks? _____

_____

4. Explain what you think Cohan is saying in the chorus. _____

_____

NAME _____ DATE _____

HOW TO RECOGNIZE PROPAGANDA

Apply Critical Thinking Skills

DIRECTIONS: Look at the illustration at the right. Then answer the questions that follow.

TEAM WORK WINS!

Your work here makes their work over there possible

With your help they are invincible
Without it they are helpless

1. To whom is this poster addressed?

_____

2. What points are being made by this poster?

_____

_____

_____

3. What arguments are being used to make these points?

_____

_____

4. How does the poster illustration help make its point?

_____

_____

5. What actions do those who created the poster hope people will take?

_____

_____

6. How would this poster influence you, if you were a worker?

_____

_____

Harcourt Brace School Publishers

Use after reading Chapter 17, Skill Lesson, pages 532–533.

The United States and the World

Connect Main Ideas

DIRECTIONS: Use this organizer to show that you understand how the chapter's main ideas are connected. Complete the organizer by writing a sentence or two about each place, event, or idea.

The United States and the World

Building an Empire

Alaska _____
_____
_____

Hawaii _____
_____
_____
_____

The Spanish-American War
_____
_____
_____

The Panama Canal
_____
_____
_____

Progressives and Reforms

The Square Deal _____
_____
_____
_____

State Government _____
_____
_____
_____

City Government _____
_____
_____
_____

Civil Rights _____
_____
_____
_____

The Great War

Allied Powers _____
_____
_____

Central Powers _____
_____
_____

The U.S. Declares War
_____
_____
_____

The League of Nations
_____
_____
_____

Use after reading Chapter 17, pages 514–535.

WHO'S DRIVING?

Interpret a Chart

DIRECTIONS: Study the chart below. Then complete the activities that follow.

FAMOUS U.S. AUTO AND TRUCK MAKERS				
NAME	**YEARS LIVED**	**HERITAGE**	**VEHICLE NAME**	**INTERESTING FACTS**
Louis Chevrolet	1879–1941	Swiss	Chevrolet	Drove a race car and worked as a car mechanic. Founded Chevrolet in 1911 with William Durant.
Henry Ford	1863–1947	Irish	Ford	Manufactured the Model T, a car that working people could afford. Started company with $28,000 of other people's money.
Augustus Mack	1873–1940	German	Mack Truck	Made truck used in WWI. Nicknamed Bulldog. Phrase *built like a Mack truck* coined from how well truck withstood use in war.
Ransom Eli Olds	1864–1950	English	Oldsmobile	Mass-produced Oldsmobiles four years before Ford sold first car. Known as *Father of the Popular-priced Car.*

1. Determine how long each person lived, and write your answers in the Years Lived column. Circle the dates of the person who lived the longest.

2. Underline the name of the person who was the first to mass-produce cars.

3. Put a star next to the vehicle that was used in World War I.

4. Use the information in the chart to decide how the early vehicle makers were similar. Then write the similarities on the blank lines below.

   a) Years Lived: _____

   b) Heritage: _____

   c) Vehicle Names: _____

DIRECTIONS: Choose one of the people mentioned in the chart. On a separate sheet of paper, write a paragraph about this person using the information from the chart.

Use after reading Chapter 18, Lesson 1, pages 537–541.

NAME _____ DATE _____

Unemployment: *1934*

Interpret Information on a Map

DIRECTIONS: The map below shows what percentage of each state's population was receiving unemployment relief in 1934. Study the map. Then complete the activities that follow.

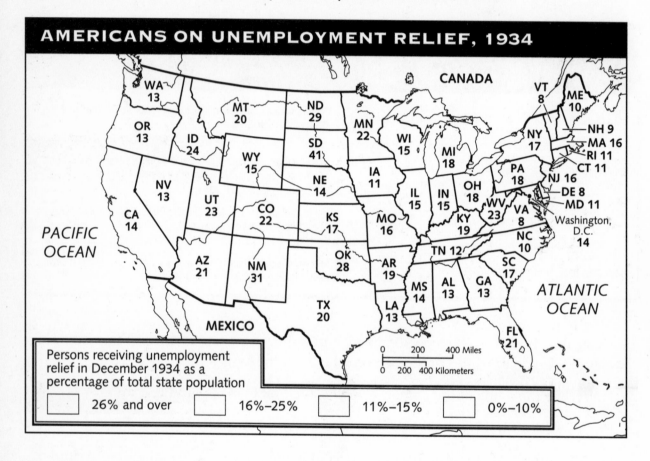

1. Select a color for each of the categories shown in the map key. Then, using the appropriate color, shade in the states that belong in each category.

2. Count the number of states for each category in the map key.

   a) Write each total next to the appropriate key box for each category.

   b) Draw a box around the key box of the category with the fewest states.

   c) Circle the key box of the category with the most states.

3. Why do you think Alaska and Hawaii are not shown on this map?

_____

Use after reading Chapter 18, Lesson 2, pages 542–546.

Harcourt Brace School Publishers

MAPPING LITERATURE

Complete a Story Map

DIRECTIONS: After reading Children of the Dust Bowl *in your textbook, complete the following story map to help organize what you have read. You may wish to copy the story map onto a separate sheet of paper.*

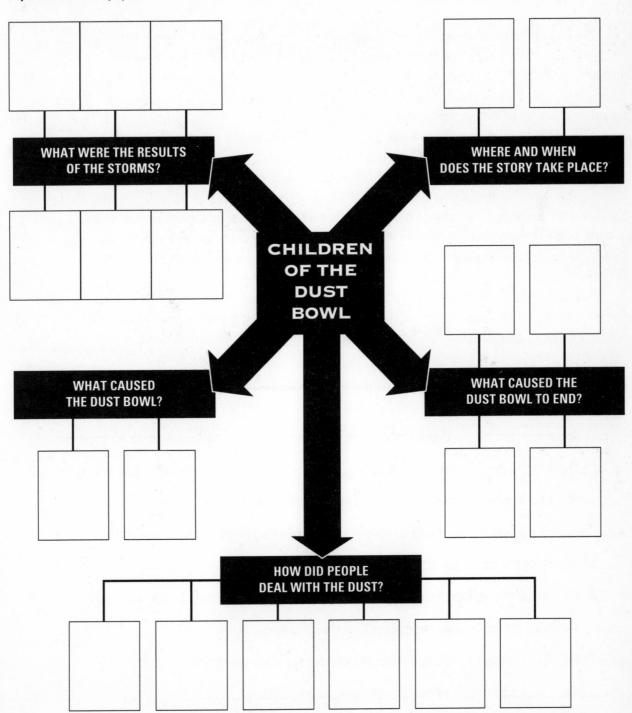

Use after reading Chapter 18, Lesson 3, pages 547–550.

Navajo Code Talkers

Distinguish Between Fact and Opinion

DIRECTIONS: Read the information below about Navajo code talkers. Then determine which of the statements that follow are based on facts and which are based on opinions. Write F next to the facts and O next to the opinions.

Secret communication is important to winning wars. If the enemy breaks secret codes, there are no surprise attacks. During World War II, codes were broken quickly by using charts based on the number of times letters are used in a language. But when the United States used Navajo code talkers, the country had an unbreakable code.

The Navajo language is difficult to learn, especially for adults. By 1940 fewer than 30 people outside the tribe knew it! The Navajo language has no written form. Different syllables and tones have different meanings based on the Navajo worldview. Four tones of voice—low, high, rising, and falling—are part of the language's sounds. About 400 Navajo volunteers served as Marine Corps code talkers during World War II. Because the code was never broken, Navajo code talkers continued to help the United States in the Korean and Vietnam wars.

Navajo code talkers were very important to the war effort. Military experts believe that code talkers shortened the war in the Pacific by at least a year. Others believe that the United States might not have won without them.

_____ **1.** The code talkers kept communication secret, which is the most important key to winning a war.

_____ **2.** Frequency charts allowed codes other than the Navajo code to be broken.

_____ **3.** The Navajo language is difficult for many people, especially adults, to learn.

_____ **4.** The Navajo language is based on four tones of voice.

_____ **5.** World War II would have ended differently without the code talkers.

_____ **6.** There is no written form of Navajo.

_____ **7.** The code talkers made the most valuable contribution to the war effort.

_____ **8.** Navajo code talkers served in several wars.

_____ **9.** The Navajo language is based on the Navajo worldview.

_____ **10.** The code talkers shortened the war by a year.

Use after reading Chapter 18, Lesson 4, pages 551–556.

WORLD WAR II NEWS

Outline News Stories

DIRECTIONS: When newspaper reporters write nonfiction stories, they answer the questions: Who? What? When? Where? Why? and How? Before reporters write, they outline the answers to these six questions. Study the outlines below, and fill in the missing information.

WHO? _____

WHAT? D day

WHEN? _____

WHERE? _____

WHY? _____

HOW? Across English Channel and landing on the beaches

WHO? _____

WHAT? _____

WHEN? August 6, 1945

WHERE? _____

WHY? _____

HOW? U.S. bomber *Enola Gay*

WHO? _____

WHAT? _____

WHEN? December 7, 1941

WHERE? _____

WHY? To damage U.S. Pacific fleet

HOW? _____

Harcourt Brace School Publishers

Use after reading Chapter 18, Lesson 5, pages 557–562.

HOW TO READ Parallel Time Lines

Apply Time Line Skills

DIRECTIONS: Use Unit 9 of your textbook to find the year each of the following events took place. Write the year in the space provided. Then, if the event is not related to World War II, write the letter of the event on the appropriate date above the time line. Write the letters of all war-related events at the appropriate places below the time line.

____ **A.** D day

____ **B.** United States enters World War II

____ **C.** Bombing of Hiroshima and Nagasaki

____ **D.** First commercial radio station broadcast

____ **E.** Japanese Americans relocated

____ **F.** Babe Ruth hits his sixtieth home run

____ **G.** First flight at Kitty Hawk

____ **H.** Nazi party takes over German government

____ **I.** Japanese attack Pearl Harbor

____ **J.** V-E Day

____ **K.** Stock market crash

____ **L.** World War II begins

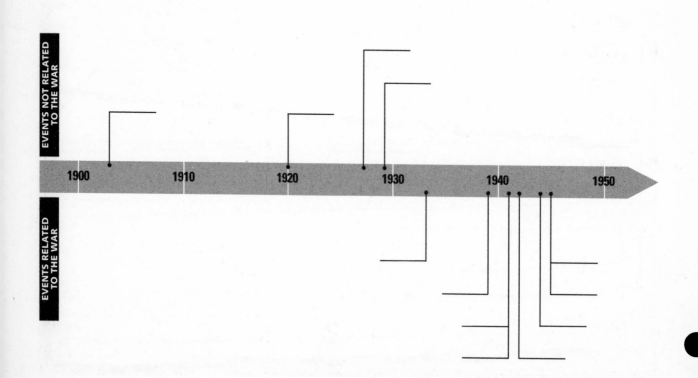

EVENTS NOT RELATED TO THE WAR

1900　1910　1920　1930　1940　1950

EVENTS RELATED TO THE WAR

Harcourt Brace School Publishers

Use after reading Chapter 18, Skill Lesson, page 563.

Good Times and Bad

Connect Main Ideas

DIRECTIONS: Use this organizer to show that you understand how the chapter's main ideas are connected. Complete the organizer by writing one or two sentences to summarize each idea or event.

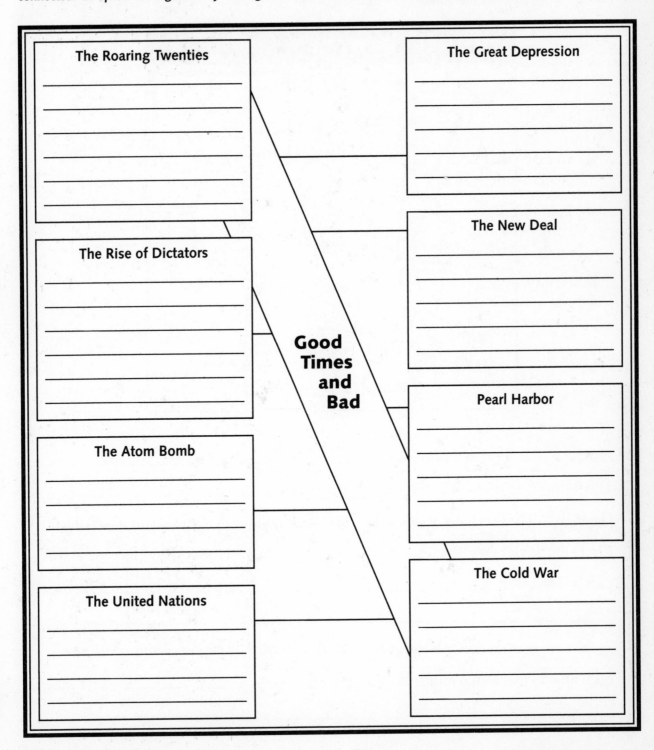

The Roaring Twenties

The Great Depression

The Rise of Dictators

The New Deal

**Good
Times
and
Bad**

The Atom Bomb

Pearl Harbor

The United Nations

The Cold War

Use after reading Chapter 18, pages 536–565.

THE BERLIN WALL

Map Skill *Read a Map*

**DIRECTIONS: Study the historical map of the Berlin Wall below.
Then complete the activities that follow.**

1. In which country was Berlin located? _____

2. The Berlin Wall divided Berlin into what two parts? _____

3. Using two different colors, shade in East and West Berlin. Fill in the key to match the map.

4. Circle the Soviet War Memorial on the map. Why do you think it was located in this

    part of Berlin? _____

    _____

5. Trace a route from Police Headquarters to the Reichstag. Would most people have

    been able to travel this route? Why? _____

    _____

Use after reading Chapter 19, Lesson 1, pages 577–581.

Harcourt Brace School Publishers

The FIRST MOon Landing

Plot a Story

DIRECTIONS: Reread the selection One Giant Leap on pages 582–587 in your textbook. Fill in the beginning, middle, and end of the story on the organizer below. Include any roadblocks, or problems, faced and solved by the characters.

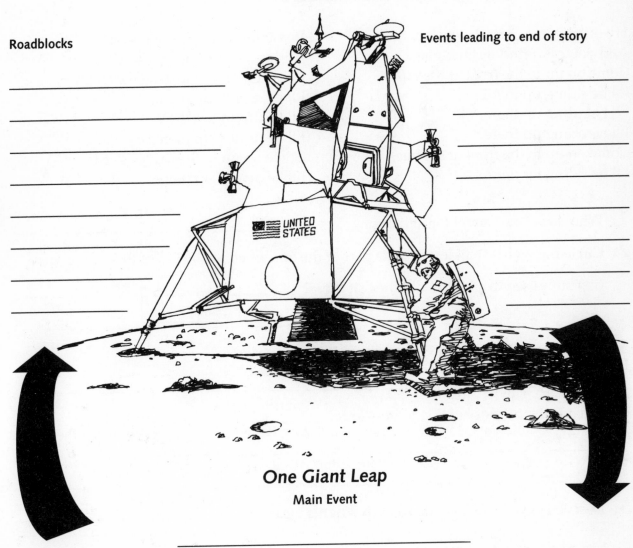

• **MIDDLE**

High Point _____

Roadblocks   Events leading to end of story

_____   _____

_____   _____

_____   _____

_____   _____

_____   _____

_____   _____

One Giant Leap
Main Event

_____

• **BEGINNING**   • **END**

_____   _____

_____   _____

Sing About CIVIL RIGHTS

Link Music to History

DIRECTIONS: Read the words to the following civil rights song "If You Miss Me from the Back of the Bus." Then complete the activities that follow.

If you miss me from the back of the bus,
And you can't find me nowhere,
Come on up to the front of the bus,
I'll be riding up there,
I'll be riding up there,
I'll be riding up there.
Come on up to the front of the bus,
I'll be riding up there.

If you miss me from the front of the bus,
And you can't find me nowhere,
Come on up to the driver's seat,
I'll be drivin' up there.
I'll be drivin' up there,
I'll be drivin' up there,
Come on up to the driver's seat,
I'll be drivin' up there.

1. Who does "me" stand for in the song? _____

2. Circle the words that describe the part of the bus where members of this group were <u>first</u> supposed to sit. Why did they sit there? _____

_____

3. In the second verse of the song, who is in the driver's seat?

_____

4. What is the purpose of this protest song? _____

_____

_____

5. Describe in your own words what civil rights mean to you. _____

_____

_____

_____

Use after reading Chapter 19, Lesson 3, pages 588–592.

HOW TO ACT AS A RESPONSIBLE CITIZEN

Apply Writing Skills

DIRECTIONS: An effective way to be a responsible citizen is to write a letter to an elected official about an issue that concerns you. On a separate sheet of paper, write a letter using the format below.

Heading —— 423 Happy Trail
Your return address and the date Nice Town, TX 77111
May 22, 1999

The President
The White House —— **Inside Address**
Washington, D.C. 20500 *Name and title of person being addressed and mailing address*

Dear Mr. President: —— **Greeting**
Make sure you properly address the person. Officials are addressed by specific titles such as "The Honorable," "Governor," or "Mayor." If you do not know the specific name and title of the person you are addressing, research it. Use a colon (:) for business letters and a comma (,) for personal letters.

Body
State your purpose in the first sentence. If you are writing for or against a certain cause, identify it and state your position at the beginning of the letter. Stick to one cause per letter. Keep it short and polite. If you write to a legislator other than your own, send a copy of your letter to your own representative. This is considered good manners and might persuade your representative to help.

Sincerely yours, —— **Closing**
Show respect by using "Sincerely yours" or "Respectfully yours."

John Q. Public
John Q. Public —— **Signature**
Type or print your name below your handwritten signature.

Use after reading Chapter 19, Skill Lesson, page 593.

MAYA LIN

Edit a Story

DIRECTIONS: Read the following story about Maya Lin. The story has some mistakes in it. Use the proofreader's marks shown in the box below to edit, or make changes to, the story.

PROOFREADER'S MARKS

MARK	MEANING	EXAMPLE
¶	make new paragraph	
℘	take out, or delete, something	the͜e time is
∧	add, or insert, something	We go∧class. *to*
/	make lowercase letter	my Ｍother
≡	capitalize, or make uppercase letter	mr. President ≡
∿	transpose letters or words	Daer

Have you had a chance to visit the Vietnam Veterans Memorial in washington, D.C.? The memorial is a simple, black granite wall. It is covered with thousands of namess of Americans who lost their lives in the war. this memorial one is of Maya Lin's most well-known designs. Her entry, number 1,026 out of 1,420 entries, won the contest to design the Vietnam Veterans memorial. She was a 21-year-old student at Yale University when she won won! Later, as an Architect, Lin was asked to desing the Civil Rights Memorial in Montgomery, alabama. This memorial is also made of black granite, But appears to float in the air. It has water flowing evenly slowly across its surface. Beneath the water, the names and events that tell the history of the civil rights movement are etched in stone. lin captured the spirit of the civil rights Movement with this monument.

Lin believes that the vietnam Veterans Memorial and the Civil Rights memorial are special. They helped our country heal some histroical wounds. She says, "If you don't remember history accurately, how can you learn"

Use after reading Chapter 19, Lesson 4, pages 594–597.

Harcourt Brace School Publishers

THE COLD WAR ERA

Place Events in Historical Context

DIRECTIONS: In the space provided, write the date of each of the following events. Then draw a line from the event to the name of the person who was President at the time the event took place.

_____ **1.** The North Korean army invades South Korea.

_____ **2.** The Cuban Missile Crisis occurs.

_____ **3.** The *Eagle* lands on the moon.

_____ **4.** Rosa Parks is arrested for sitting in the wrong section of a bus.

_____ **5.** Sandra Day O'Connor is appointed to the U.S. Supreme Court.

_____ **6.** South Vietnam surrenders to North Vietnam.

_____ **7.** The Vietnam Veterans Memorial opens to visitors.

_____ **8.** The President visits communist China.

_____ **9.** The Soviet Union invades Afghanistan.

_____ **10.** Germans tear down the Berlin Wall.

Lyndon B. Johnson

Gerald Ford

Richard M. Nixon

Harry S. Truman

Dwight D. Eisenhower

Ronald Reagan

John F. Kennedy

Jimmy Carter

George Bush

HOW TO UNDERSTAND Political Symbols

The Odd Couple

Marco Polo

(Continued)

Use after reading Chapter 19, Skill Lesson, page 605.

NAME _____ DATE _____

Apply Visual Thinking Skills

DIRECTIONS: Study the cartoons on page 128. Then complete the following activities.

1. One of the most widely used political symbols representing the United States is the eagle. The bear is a political symbol representing the Soviet Union. The cartoon titled "The Odd Couple" appeared in the newspaper in 1973. Why do you think the United States and the Soviet Union were called the "odd couple"?

   _____

   _____

2. Circle another political symbol on the cartoon that represents the United States. Circle one that represents the Soviet Union.

3. "The Odd Couple" cartoon symbolizes détente between the United States and the Soviet Union. Using the cartoon and the information in your textbook, write your own definition

   of détente. _____

   _____

4. What does the dove in the baby carriage symbolize? _____

5. In February 1972, President Nixon made his historic visit to the People's Republic of China. In the cartoon titled "Marco Polo," circle the political symbol that shows that Nixon was a member of the Republican party. Put a box around the political symbol that shows that Nixon represented the United States.

6. What does the cartoon show Nixon bringing into China, and what do these things

   represent? _____

   _____

   _____

DIRECTIONS: Choose a topic from this chapter. Then, on a separate sheet of paper, illustrate that topic by using political symbols.

Harcourt Brace School Publishers

The United States in the Cold War Years

Connect Main Ideas

DIRECTIONS: Use this organizer to show that you understand how the chapter's main ideas are connected. Complete the organizer by writing the main idea of each lesson.

The United States in the Cold War Years

The Cold War Begins

_____

_____

_____

One Giant Leap

_____

_____

_____

_____

_____

The Struggle for Equal Rights

_____

_____

_____

_____

_____

_____

War in Vietnam and Protests at Home

_____

_____

_____

_____

_____

The Cold War Ends and New Challenges Begin

_____

_____

_____

Use after reading Chapter 19, pages 576–607.

Comparing NAFTA Countries

Read a Table

DIRECTIONS: Examine the table below to see how the NAFTA countries compare in various categories. Then answer the questions that follow.

COMPARE COUNTRIES			
	CANADA	**UNITED STATES**	**MEXICO**
Population	28,114,000	260,714,000	92,202,000
Growth rate (1990–2000)	1.2%	1.0%	1.9%
Telephones per 100 people	59	56	8
Newspapers per 1,000 people	228	249	133
Televisions per 1,000 people	639	814	147

1. Which country has the largest population? _____

2. Which country's population is growing at the fastest rate? _____

3. Which categories shown in the table reflect means of communications?

   _____

4. Which country has the most telephones per 100 people? _____

5. How many telephones per 100 people are there in the United States?

   _____

6. Which country has the fewest newspapers per 1,000 people?

   _____

7. Which country has the most newspapers per 1,000 people?

   _____

8. How many more televisions per 1,000 people does the United States have than Mexico?

   _____

Harcourt Brace School Publishers

SAVE THE RAIN FOREST

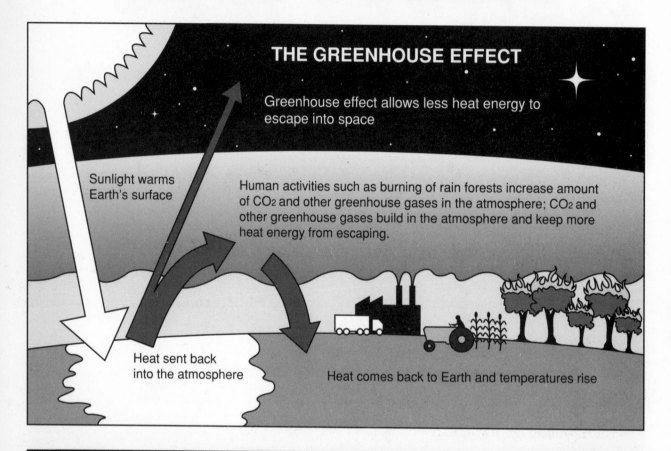

THE GREENHOUSE EFFECT

Greenhouse effect allows less heat energy to escape into space

Sunlight warms Earth's surface

Human activities such as burning of rain forests increase amount of CO_2 and other greenhouse gases in the atmosphere; CO_2 and other greenhouse gases build in the atmosphere and keep more heat energy from escaping.

Heat sent back into the atmosphere

Heat comes back to Earth and temperatures rise

GREENHOUSE GASES AND THEIR SOURCES

GREENHOUSE GAS	SOURCES	LIFE SPAN IN ATMOSPHERE
carbon dioxide (CO_2)	fossil fuels, deforestation, soil destruction	500 years
chlorofluorocarbons (CFCs 11 and 12)	refrigeration, air conditioning, aerosols, foam blowing, solvents	65 to 110 years
methane (CH_4)	cattle, rice paddies, gas leaks, mining, termites	7 to 10 years
nitrous oxide (N_2O)	fossil fuels, soil cultivation, deforestation	140 to 190 years
ozone and other trace gases	photochemical processes, gasoline-powered vehicles, power plants, solvents	hours to days

(Continued)

NAME _____ DATE _____

DIRECTIONS: Study the diagram on page 132. Then complete the activities that follow.

1. Follow the arrow from the sun to the Earth's surface. What happens when the sunlight hits the Earth's surface? _____

    _____

2. Follow the split arrow leaving the Earth's surface. What barrier does it hit?

    _____

    _____

3. Read the caption and study the illustrations in the diagram that show what causes this barrier. Describe what you think causes it. _____

    _____

    _____

4. Follow the split arrow to its two ends. List the results produced by the greenhouse effect.

    _____

    _____

DIRECTIONS: Study the chart on page 132. Then complete the activities that follow.

5. Circle the greenhouse gases that are produced by the destruction of the rain forests.

6. Put an **X** through the name of the greenhouse gas that takes the longest to disappear from the atmosphere.

7. Put a check mark next to the two greenhouse gases that are produced by fossil fuels.

8. Underline the greenhouse gas produced by automobiles.

9. Study the diagram and the chart. Write a paragraph on a separate sheet of paper describing specific things that you can do to help stop the greenhouse effect.

HOW TO USE POPULATION MAPS

Apply Map Skills

DIRECTIONS: The size of each state shown on this map is based on the population of the state and not the area, or geographic size, of the state. Examine this map and compare it to the map of the United States on page A8 in your textbook. Then answer the questions on page 135.

CARTOGRAM: POPULATION OF THE UNITED STATES

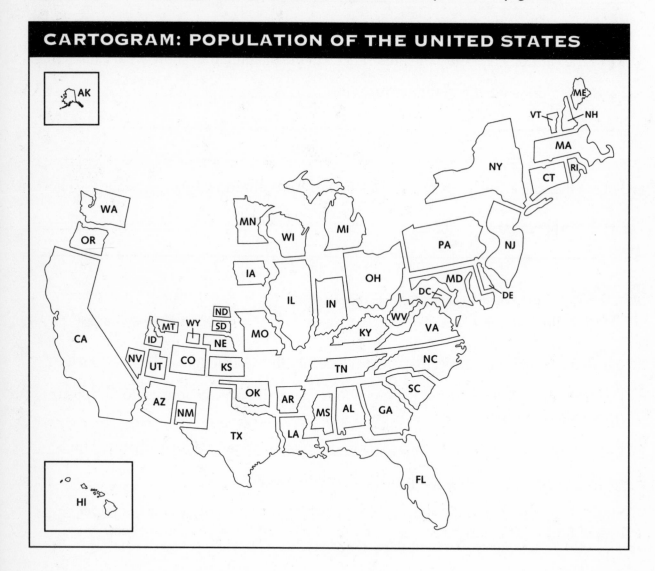

Harcourt Brace School Publishers

(Continued)

Use after reading Chapter 20, Skill Lesson, pages 618–619.

1. Look at the map on page A8 of your textbook. What is the largest state in the United States? _____

2. Why does the cartogram on page 134 show California as the largest state?

   _____

   _____

3. Can you tell from the cartogram which is the largest state in the United States in terms of geographic size? Why? _____

   _____

   _____

4. What are the five most populated states in the United States?

   _____

5. Which state has the larger population—New Jersey or Washington?

   _____

6. The population of Ohio is about how many times greater than the population of the state of Washington? _____

7. If the population of the state of Washington is about 5,500,000, about what is the population of Ohio? _____

8. Of the following three states which two are closest in population, Pennsylvania, Illinois or Indiana? _____

9. Give an example to illustrate that the cartogram shows relative populations of the states and not exact population numbers for them. _____

   _____

   _____

   _____

10. Color in your state on the cartogram on page 134.

Harcourt Brace School Publishers

Country Card Catalog

Identify Countries in the Caribbean and in Central America

DIRECTIONS: Use the map on page 621 in your textbook and an almanac to help you complete the country cards that follow. Color in the main parts of the flags as accurately as possible.

Country Name: _____

Capital: _____

Shares Borders with (Country Names): _____

Country Fact: _____

_____

Country Name: _____

Capital: _____

Shares Borders with (Country Names): _____

_____

Country Fact: _____

Country Name: _____

Capital: _____

Shares Borders with (Country Names): _____

Country Fact: _____

_____

(Continued)

Harcourt Brace School Publishers

Use after reading Chapter 20, Lesson 3, pages 620–624.

Country Name: _____

Capital: _____

Shares Borders with (Country Names): _____

Country Fact: _____

_____

Country Name: _____

Capital: _____

Shares Borders with (Country Names): _____

_____

Country Fact: _____

Country Name: _____

Capital: _____

Shares Borders with (Country Names): _____

Country Fact: _____

_____

TROPICAL RAIN FORESTS

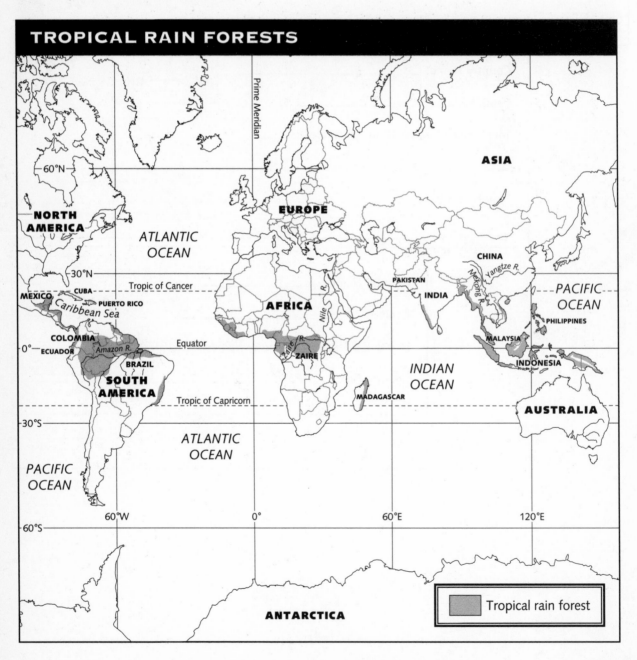

Interpret a Resource Map

DIRECTIONS: Study the map of tropical rain forests on this page. Then complete the activities that follow.

TROPICAL RAIN FORESTS

ASIA

NORTH AMERICA

ATLANTIC OCEAN

60°N

30°N

Tropic of Cancer

MEXICO   CUBA
Caribbean Sea   PUERTO RICO

COLOMBIA
ECUADOR   Amazon R.   Equator

BRAZIL

SOUTH AMERICA

Tropic of Capricorn

30°S

ATLANTIC OCEAN

PACIFIC OCEAN

60°S

EUROPE

Prime Meridian

AFRICA

Nile R.

Zaire R.
ZAIRE

MADAGASCAR

CHINA

Yangtze R.

PAKISTAN

Mekong R.

INDIA

PACIFIC OCEAN

PHILIPPINES

MALAYSIA

INDONESIA

INDIAN OCEAN

AUSTRALIA

ANTARCTICA

60°W   0°   60°E   120°E

Tropical rain forest

(Continued)

1. Draw an **X** through the names of the continents that have no tropical rain forests.

2. Draw a circle around the names of the three continents that have the most tropical rain forests.

3. Underline the name of the country in which deforestation has left many American Indians homeless.

4. List the reasons for deforestation of this country. _____

_____

5. Which three rivers flow through tropical rain forests? _____

_____

6. Between which two special lines of latitude are most of the tropical rain forests located?

_____

7. Why do you think most tropical rain forests lie between these two lines of latitude?

_____

_____

_____

8. What line of latitude passes through rain forests in Brazil, Zaire and Malaysia?

_____

9. Are there any tropical rain forests north of 60° N latitude? _____

10. Are there any tropical rain forests north of 60° S latitude? _____

11. Are there any tropical rain forests shown in the continental United States?

_____

Harcourt Brace School Publishers

Canada

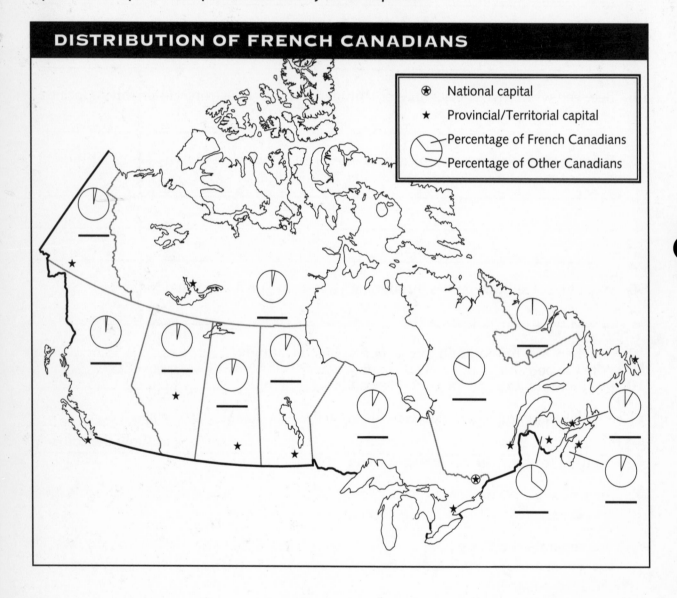

Apply Information from a Table to a Map

DIRECTIONS: Use the map on page 629 in your textbook to help you to label Canada's capital and the capital of each province and territory on the map below.

DISTRIBUTION OF FRENCH CANADIANS

⊛ National capital

★ Provincial/Territorial capital

Percentage of French Canadians

Percentage of Other Canadians

Harcourt Brace School Publishers

(Continued)

DIRECTIONS: Use the information in the table below to complete the activities that follow.

CANADA		
PROVINCE/TERRITORY	**FRENCH CANADIANS** (in percentages)	**OTHERS** (in percentages)
Newfoundland	0.6	
Prince Edward Island	8.6	
Nova Scotia	6.1	
New Brunswick	35.9	
Quebec	82.5	
Ontario	7.4	
Manitoba	7.0	
Saskatchewan	4.4	
Alberta	3.6	
British Columbia	1.7	
Northwest Territories	3.4	
Yukon Territory	3.6	

1. Write the percentage of French Canadians in each province and territory from the above table on the appropriate write-on lines on the map on page 140.

2. Color or shade each circle graph to show the percentage of French Canadians in each province and territory on the map on page 140. Fill in the key box to show the color you used to show the percentage of French Canadians.

3. Determine the percentage of other groups living in each province and territory. Write this percentage in the appropriate column in the above table.

4. On a separate sheet of paper, write a paragraph summarizing why Quebec would want to separate from Canada. Use the information on the map, in the table, and in your textbook to help you.

THE WESTERN HEMISPHERE TODAY

Connect Main Ideas

DIRECTIONS: Use this organizer to show that you understand how the chapter's main ideas are connected. Complete the organizer by writing the main idea of each lesson.

The Western Hemisphere Today

Mexico Today

_____
_____
_____
_____
_____
_____

The Peoples of Canada

_____
_____
_____
_____
_____
_____

Democracy in the Caribbean and in Central America

_____
_____
_____
_____

Challenges in South America

_____
_____
_____
_____
_____

Harcourt Brace School Publishers